# By Blood, By Moon

## Other works by Heather E. Hutsell:

"Awakening Alice" as featured in *Ghost on the Highway*

*Awakening Alice ~\*~ A Ticket for Patience*

*The Inter-Twinning*

*The Labyrinth of Empty*

# By Blood, By Moon

## By

## Heather E. Hutsell

*By Blood, By Moon*
Copyright 2009
1st edition

It is to my greatest regret that this is a work of fiction and all
characters and events here within do not exist.

ISBN 978-0-578-04769-0

For Alexander ~

For the beast you made of me…

For Matthew~

Because you were willing to become the beast…

# Chapter One

Elena ran until her lungs began to burn, obsessing all the while about what she thought she had seen, and scarcely remembering at the same time how to breathe. It was the blackest part of night and she needed to stop before her heart became a tighter and everlasting knot. She needed to rest, to gain back her wits and make some sense over the abrupt events that had awakened her with their clamor. It had caused her to rise quickly from her own bed, her head spinning from the forcing off of sleep, before she peeked into the adjacent room. And the cause had been there, seeming so much a dream itself, and she had narrowly escaped the repercussions of her curiosity. But *it* had seen her—there was no mistaking that it had—and the sharp pinning of its eyes had promised that it would be after her next.

But even as she ran, she wanted to argue that it was not real—very much so had she wanted to find it to just be part of an absurd imprint of a dream she had had. *Surely* she had just dreamed it all—? And never minding that it had appeared haunting and strangely surreal and the movements seemed impossible: for how long had she claimed to see ghosts? Starting with her mother's demise and reappearance and ever since, always Elena had the knowing that she was not alone. Was this just simply not another of those presences? It had been for too many of her nearly thirty years of age that she had had this. It was this very recurring sort of incident, this *affliction* that had prompted her father to send her away when she was much younger—she was knowing this now, and much too late was it all becoming clear.

But the ghosts had been real and fleeting and harmless—and this had been far from any sort of ghost. It had seemed to be alive and breathing and solid, and it hungered as a living thing should, and it devoured as a living thing— though *not human*, she caught herself thinking—might. But it also moved in a way as no human could and still Elena's eyes told her that it was exactly that.

She paused to try to settle her breaths, for it was becoming hard to think rationally and her eyes strained to focus on the swimming scenery around her. She was going to have to determine which direction to the sea would be safest, and she hoped fastest, but Elena frowned deeply as none of her options seemed to be either, not knowing exactly what it was that she was running from. She resorted to pushing on next to the wide river, the trees keeping dense along side of her.

The creature—for what else could it have been? came again to mind. She had not seen others, but was certain *it* had not been alone. And its hunger—for she could not stop thinking of its horrific display— was very different from a man's. Elena tried to reason that men could not shred the flesh of other men without weapons used, nor did they savor the blood of human victims and then slip into shadow until the hunger beckoned they come out once again. She knew of the sort of things that did this—she had learned it, had pondered the idea of it, but never expected such a thing to be real, and in front of her face. At this realization, she knew that she could be safe nowhere, but fatigue was growing on Elena and would not let her reach the port without another short rest. She gave in, crouching with her back to the river and ready to move if she had to. And though she knew it would be quite useless against what was now hunting her, she held her sword ready and waiting.

Whoever—or *whatever* had been attacking the people of her village had been very precise and quite selective about it: the victims consisting only of her brother, her two uncles and her father—and no one else. If the murders had been acts of vengeance, she could think up no motives, for her family was held in high regard by all who knew them. But if it was for the simple sake of wiping out her bloodline, then certainly these beasts were making swift progress. She wondered if she had lured the killer into her village with her return—it had been a mere week ago for it, and when the murders without delay had begun. But why now? She had been gone for so many years! What would her return have had to do with it? Elena had made many acquaintances while she had been parted from her family, but certainly she had not associated with anyone who might have felt the need in doing away with her lineage.

She knew that she had locked eyes with the creature that night, and he had marked her. Only by the distraction of blade and bullet from loyal friends to her family had she escaped the house.

A far off howl interrupting her thoughts like a siren made every nerve in her jump, and she began at once to run again, the brief rest now having to have been enough.

She reached a short dock off of the river and a small boat was fast tied to it. There was no hesitation as she climbed in, freeing it by means of her quick-cutting blade and she began to row as quickly as she could with the current. Not far from that point, she knew the river would open up into the sea and she would soon find the port, and there her chance for escape would be greater. Elena glanced back now and then, but nothing save the dark trees were there. It was a very deep sigh that brought her paddling to a pause, her eyes closing for only seconds. She opened them again, catching a flash of white in the passing trees. She dared not breathe, her eyes searching frantically, straining in the darkness to be certain that she was only seeing images brought on by a tired mind. But the wind was blowing the heavy clouds in to create a thicker darkness and she was again paddling away. The outlet to the sea was becoming near, but as she rounded the embankment, she found that the figure of a man stood there, watching her, waiting. Her heart froze along with her movements and the traitorous current took her right for him.

She was drawn up before the young man who stood like a statue but for his intensely gazing blue eyes. He was dressed simply with his white peasant shirt tattered and open, his black trousers in a similarly ragged state. He wore no shoes, the unshaven scruff on his sweetly handsome face showed signs of a coming beard, and his dark, disheveled hair caught on the wind and blew across his eyes. None of this did he seem to notice, and Elena was quite positive that he did not notice anything but her, for the pinning of his eyes did not stray from her for a single moment.

The boat lodged itself onto the mud, the man now only a few feet away. He was not one of *them*—could not be, she reasoned, for there was no blood on him. And never, without horse or other rapid means could he have possibly caught up with her, undetected until now.

He reached his hand out to her at once and she raised her blade in quick response.

"You must come with me, if you do not wish to become like the rest of your family—" he said at this. She hesitated a moment more—if only at his blunt choice of words, but something in his eyes prompted her up onto land. She avoided his offered hand, but her eyes never left him for a second.

"I am William." And at his introduction, Elena's suspicion of him lessened slightly, not thinking her own true killer would bother with any sort of formality—certainly the one back in her home had not afforded her father the sentiment. "Lady, you do not have much time."

She gave in and hurried along with him through the woods, his sight in the darkness very acute where she could scarcely see her own hand in front of her face. She wondered if the branches and brambles that snapped under her shod feet were cutting him up terribly, for the very sound of them and the scraping she endured on her arms and cheeks smarted too much for her to ignore. He gave no indication that he felt a thing—he nearly floated over the ground and his agility-graced speed was clearly reined for her sake.

"Where do you take me?"

"Somewhere safer."

"And that would be—?"

"To speak of it would not be wise. Keep your gait."

"But, I know nothing about you—and you ask me to follow—how should I know to trust—?"

He stopped suddenly and turned to her, holding her with his eyes as they nearly collided. She wavered slightly under their fierceness, as clearly they claimed a beast inside, but they were also passionate, protective and full of fire.

"You question your trust of me, and still you follow. Had I wanted to end your life, little one, I could have already and you would have been none the wiser for it."

Elena's protest caught in her throat but she could not stop the inelegance of her words.

"I only meant that I have no knowledge of you—after what I just saw happening to my people— I have never before seen you—" She was stammering. "How do you know me? Why do you help?" And as the shock and fear was waning, realization of the slaughter was coming alive in her senses, and rising up from her chest in uncomfortable, ragged breaths.

"My lady," he began with a softer tone. "Everyone for days' worth of miles around here knows of you."

"And now you are here to protect me—"

"I am trying to accomplish something to that effect."

"Why you?"

"We do not have time for that now. Another time, perhaps, if you survive this night."

And he continued on, Elena following as closely behind as she could. They began to hasten their steps evermore and found themselves running, Elena's sudden and graceless stumble happening fast and William's turning and catching of her even faster. She caught her breath, finding herself in his arms and their faces very close, the smell of him strong and sweet.

"Watch your step, Elena." His voice was soft and his hold on her gentle, but she could feel the strength of him very clearly.

"Thank you, William." She whispered her words, a little shocked at hearing him speak her name so informally.

It began to rain as they resumed their run, his hand now securely and urgently holding hers. She kept up well enough but Elena was beginning to feel numb, her entire life and the world around her feeling as though it all belonged to someone else, though a part of her felt that she wanted to crumple under the grief of it all. William felt it in her and his hand gently tightened around hers.

"Not far now—"

And as promised, it was not long before they stepped out of the trees and stood at the top of a perilously steep hill. Below them lay the port and the neighboring village Elena had been trying to get to. She turned to William, most grateful and knowing he had saved her most of the night, and for this: her very life.

"Go now," he instructed, though he was as hesitant to let go of her hand as she was of his. "You should be safe from here. I will watch until you are aboard the ship that awaits you."

"You'll not follow—?" At their words, it struck Elena that their brief acquaintance was suddenly far too brief to her.

"As I would like nothing more," he began. "You and all others would be safer at this time did I not."

"Safer—?" She backed a step away, her hand still caught and she tried wrenching it away. "You *are* one of them?"

"*No*! Not one of *them*!" He was insistent on it, but Elena heard the catch in his tone, the release coming. "But still, you would not be free from danger, did I remain at your side."

11

"There is no time for further answers from you, is there?"

"Go, Elena—*please*—"

"Thank you, again—"

He only nodded and she hurriedly scaled down the hill, careful to stay on her feet. She only looked back once to see if William still remained—and he did, ever watching her.

The streets of the village were dim, as the entire place seemed to be sleeping. As well its inhabitants should be, she mused, for it was creeping into the twilight hours. But it was also unnaturally quiet, and not even the pub was lively. She grew uneasy at this and scurried on. But as she drew closer to the awaiting ship, a reasonless, sickening dread came over her. There really seemed to be no one around, and still there was a heavy presence very close by.

"Little Elena—"

She started at the sultry sound of her name and whipped around to the voice that had addressed her. A young gentleman stood across the way from her, the wind picking up the ends of his evergreen velvet cloak to reveal his decadent black clothing beneath. His hair was long and rakish, and shone like jet. His eyes were silver and Elena felt ensnared right into them.

"How nice of William to bring you to me," the man was praising. Hurt fury rushed into Elena for the man who had claimed to his helping of her. Her eyes went to where he had stood on the hill, but he was gone now, and in that instant, the well-dressed man had come to her back, the swiftness in his movements seeming humanly impossible. She felt his breath on her neck, his hands clamping down on hers at her sides before she could raise her sword and it was quickly dislodged from her grasp.

"Who are you?" she demanded, her voice thin.

"Do you not recognize me?" He breathed in her scent, his hair tickling against her ear and she could scarcely shake her head. "Perhaps you did not see me. But, my friend you know—"

Her eyes lifted and she saw another man waiting against a wall across the street. It was hard to see him in the shadows, but as the clouds were quickly clearing away again, he stepped forward into the light of the gas lamps and the partial moonlight, his clothing shown soiled with blood. She recognized him as the man she had seen in her father's

12

home—the apparition come to life—and the very being she had witnessed killing him. Her breath caught and she backed up into the gentleman behind her, the other grinning at her identifying of him. At this, a third showed, bloody as well.

"What now do you want? You have taken my family—they are every one of them gone now, and you hesitate to take my life. *What*?" she demanded. "What is it you want?"

Before an answer could be offered, the moon showed fully from behind the clouds, and a howl sounded close by. The men exchanged a glance and Elena's captor shoved her into the grasp of one of the others, the smell of the blood making her swoon with a turning stomach.

"Get her to the carriage. I shall deal with William."

Her jaw dropped and she glanced again at where she had last seen her guide. Still he was not there, but this drew the attention of the others.

"He is a creature, just as we are, sweet one," explained their newly arriving leader. "Though not so much like us." He nodded to her new captor, Elena trying to understand as she was taken along quickly, the source of the sudden growl now blocked from her view.

"Where do we go now?" she asked, as she was led to the mentioned carriage. "And what creatures are you—?"

Her fear of them was slightly swayed, as they seemed not quite ready to bring on her end. And that William could be anything evil or dangerous—she did not believe it. The man gripping her arm chuckled behind her as he pushed her along.

"I am Tavin—that is Marius. Nicolas is seeing to your new friend. And, my darling, we are what you would know as Vampyres. But there shall be time for formal introductions later. Much later."

A bit of her fear returned when he opened the carriage from the back and his companion lifted the lid of a rough-hewn, bare wooden casket before looking at her expectantly.

"I-is that meant for me—?" She dreaded the answer and tried to back away, but Tavin was an unmoving wall behind her.

"For now, my dear. But do try not to worry—you shall grow quite used to them. And out of necessity, you will surely find yourself longing to be in one."

"The one you will soon have shall be far more suitable for you," Marius promised.

"Most definitely more comfortable."

Tavin gave a gentle push but Elena dug her heels into the ground, shaking her head in protest.

"No—" Softly said but a strong shove came fast. Quick reflexes propelled her away and clamped-down hands on her arms stayed her.

"*No*! Please—*please*!" Cried this time, loudly. And from wherever it had sounded, the growl she had heard only moments before rumbled even more closely by.

Tavin froze and Elena turned to him, a glimmer of hope in her eyes.

"That—is *William*?"

"My dear, it seems you were quite sheltered in your far off school," Marius chided. "Probably just as your father had intended you to be. Incredible injustice, truly."

But Tavin turned her back to him, her eyes locking with his and she felt she could not move, or blink or even breathe. His fingers brushed her cheek, his eyes still holding hers. The growling seemed to come up behind him, but it all seemed so far off to Elena just then.

"So beautiful she is, William," Tavin was saying as he cupped her chin and lifted her face upward. "So full of life—it is no wonder why you desire her for yourself—"

Elena began to feel sleepy and thin and light, vaguely noting that one of the other Vampyres stood at her back, pushing closed the space between her and Tavin.

"Is she not beautiful, Marius?" Tavin was saying as the other Vampyre cleared Elena's hair away from her neck and held it in his gentle fist. "If you come any closer, William, we will turn her right now—"

And what had once been William stood on hind legs and towered up over Tavin's shoulder. The beast's golden eyes sought Elena's and though she attempted to look at him, Marius held her head still and she could not focus. His nearness made Tavin's hand slip over Elena's throat and his grip tightened, the sharp nail of his thumb testing into the vein.

"Do you wish to keep killing her?"

Elena's eyes cleared enough to see the fangs revealed by Tavin's smile and William backed down at the awakened fear in her face. So very slowly she began to feel—the figure

14

of Marius still behind her, his ice-cold breath against her neck and two pairs of hands holding her.

"She belongs to us, William. Always has—" And this came in Marius's voice.

In a breath, William stripped Tavin away and they were combating, Nicolas suddenly in his place. There was an immediate moment of icy piercing on both sides of her throat, Nicolas first and Marius following, and it was quickly replaced with searing heat as Elena felt herself melt under the biting and the drawing of her blood. She dropped to the blissful brink of death, Marius supporting her as her legs gave, and then as the clouds covered the moon, William was changed and Tavin held him more easily at bay.

"Marius, you cannot condemn her to this kind of life!" he was insisting as Nicolas was taking Elena and lifting her to place her into the rough, awaiting coffin. "She does not deserve this!"

"Can I not?" Marius challenged, still relishing the shocking taste of her blood, and scarcely able to retain his own wits from it. It was what he had expected and much of what he had not. "The change is underway, my friend. Would you now have me leave her tied to a stake instead? Awaiting the morning sun—her very end?" William did not answer, for reasons he did not know, his world needed her to survive as well. "I did not think so."

Marius nodded to his companions and they boarded the carriage, William defenseless and praying for the moon to again reveal itself.

"She will not survive the turning," William was saying. "They *never* do—"

And it was true, for Elena felt she was floating far, far away from them now, on a very black and blissful sea.

"We shall see," Marius promised. "So very soon, we shall see."

15

# Chapter Two

The heavily thudding lid echoed in Elena's head, even still as it had been removed a great while after it had closed, and she had been placed on a grand bed draped in ivory and indigo. Her senses were slowly being regained, and she felt the closeness of others, for she was not left alone. A hand lifted hers to press it to warm lips, the gesture bringing her eyes to open. She found Tavin and Nicolas lying at her sides, both of them dressed sparsely in only britches of fine silk, and both of them having been eager in awaiting Elena's awakening. She noted that her own embroidered chemise and hastily pulled on Turkish trousers had been replaced by a gown of fine, milky white muslin, the feather-lightness of it against her skin feeling instead of abrasive wool. The Vampyres felt her stir and they rose to sit above her, grinning to one another and then down at Elena.

"Good evening, beauty."

Elena felt far too weak to respond to Nicolas, and a growing, angry emptiness filled the pit of her stomach. It was a hunger that turned and toiled in her like nothing she had ever felt before, and it pained so terribly throughout her entire body, that she could think of nothing but to wish for it to end. She was not certain she wanted to die, but if it would only end the aching.

"Please—" she whispered. Tavin pressed his fingers to her lips.

"Do not speak," he instructed. "You are still— *unrestored*, and we have yet to replenish you. Exertion will surely do you in and Elena, you are so *very* close to your end."

Nicolas turned her to face him.

"Do you thirst, little one?" He asked this, knowing that she did, though Elena knew not what for. Without waiting for her answer, he drew a sharp thumb dagger across the smooth and perfect bare skin over his heart. The line filled and dropped crimson in a slow trickle toward her. She could smell the sweetness but lacked the vitality to rise up to it. Nicolas smiled again at this and drew her head up in a cradling hand, bringing her mouth to his skin. His blood dripped onto her lips, her tongue hesitant but flicking lightly over it. It tasted of life, of honeyed sweetness, hot and powerful with his heart working to push it forth with every beat. And the familiarity to her—the carrying of her own memories within each drop, built on her hunger, pushing her to take in the blood, to seal her lips to his skin and suck it out.

"Aye, beauty, that is the way," Nicolas coaxed, nearly shaking from the anticipation of it, and Elena gaining enough strength from just a few drops to lift herself up a bit. Her eyes went to his, the silver of his smiling, seducing. He slipped his thumb between her lips and parted them, her own new sharp fangs having grown. He half smiled, the fierce sinking of those fangs into the flesh he had already opened to make new punctures, catching him off guard. He gasped softly at the brutal force as she drank deeply, his arm clutching her tightly to him.

The slightly muffled sound of his moans became clearer to Elena as she drank of Nicolas. She began to feel Tavin closing in behind her, the length of him an enticing wall, and his hand was reaching around the front of her in an embrace, pulling her back against him. His gentle urging away made Elena release Nicolas, and he could scarcely speak, his own strength spent beyond the ecstasy of it.

"Tavin—have her, of you now—"

And with gentle drawing, Tavin turned Elena to face him, catching her face in his hand beneath her chin and licking the stray streams of blood from her mouth. It so enraptured him, that he began falling into a kiss with her, but Nicolas's sudden grasping of his arm and the puncturing of a vein inside Tavin's elbow drew Elena away from the yielding mouth, and to the nourishing stream opened to her. In only moments, Tavin was savoring the same explosive waves that Nicolas had, and he pulled Elena more closely and tightly to him. Moments more passed with her feeding on him, Nicolas regaining enough strength to close in on Elena and feather kisses across her shoulder and down her arm, his mouth toying with biting into her wrist, though he did not.

The exchange was interrupted when Marius entered the chamber. He approached the bed without pause, Nicolas remaining at Elena's side as she drank, Tavin still far off on currents of blissfulness. Marius looked somewhat disapproving but climbed onto the bed with them.

"You could not wait for the quickening—?"

"Marius—" Nicolas purred. "Have a turn—"

With her energies and senses now as strong as Marius's own, Elena rose from Tavin and turned to Marius as he sat back on his heels. He cupped her chin in his hand and raised her eyes to his and Elena dove into them with an eagerness that nearly knocked him back.

"Can you feed once more, my dear?"

In answer, she parted his velvet jacket, her warmed fingertips brushing over the skin of his chest. He grasped her wrists suddenly, stopping her. Elena's eyes went to his again for instruction.

"My lord—?"

One hand moved to close around her nape and he brought her to him, his words whispered against her ear.

"It has been, so long, since I was bitten here—" His mouth grazed her neck and she took the cue, her open mouth and fangs brushing his throat. "And my last quickening was so—lacking—" Elena did not wait to hear more before sinking her teeth into him, his gasp and exhale of equal pleasure to Tavin's and Nicolas's.

They rested a moment more as Marius had his turn, but then Nicolas brought Elena down onto her back, her clinging embrace bringing Marius down over her. Tavin stroked her ivory leg, his lips teasing over the skin by her ankle and Nicolas's own hands sliding up her other thigh, his thumb brushing tenderly, teasingly against her warmth.

"Marius, let us drink of her when she has done with you," Nicolas began. "So we may have her feed on us again." His tongue licked over Elena's hip and she gasped this time, ending Marius's quickening.

It was a moment before the eldest of them could find words.

"Not, tonight—" he breathed. He lifted from Elena as she smiled at him and he smiled back, pleased. "Give her rest. Give yourselves rest."

Marius was quite spent, dizzy from Elena's taking of his blood, and he closed his jacket modestly. The three of them leaned over her, silver now sparkling in the green of her eyes.

"I shall not sleep, come morn," she assured them.

"But you shall, for it is almost upon us," Marius promised. "And perhaps tomorrow night, you shall leave here to hunt."

*Hunt.* The word left a strange heaviness in her mind. Marius stood to leave the chamber.

"Get to where you shall be safe from the dawn." Tavin rose as well, kissing Elena's crown.

"Thank you—" He said no more as he smiled and left them. Marius remained at the door.

"Quickly then."

"I will show her to her berth." Nicolas had promised, looking none too pleased or patient at Marius, who then nodded, gave a long warning look and then left them as well.

When they were alone, Nicolas rested his forehead against Elena's, a mischievous smile playing in his eyes.

"Do you still thirst, my beauty?" Her eyes took his challenge.

"Do *you*?"

His grin grew wider still and his hand reached up to caress her face.

"Well—it is still a few hours until the sun rises," he began.

"But Marius said—"

"*Marius*, said—" His fingertips touched her lips, stopping her words. "I will be sure to keep you safe, my beauty." With his promise, he brought her closer to him, his mouth very near hers. "But first—"

Nicolas captured her mouth in a deep kiss, feeling in her return that none of her fear from before her turning remained. He began a trail then, from her lips to breast as he took her into the depths of the bedding. He glanced up to her face, their eyes catching.

"My turn."

Elena sucked in her breath as Nicolas's bite punctured her neck, her back arching to him until he rose up, taking her with him. He stopped drinking after only a moment, still holding her.

"So very full you are, Elena. So very sweet you taste, still as you did before. Shall I take my fill of you now? And you of me once again when I am through?"

At his words, she went to his throat, and he let her drink. He had only taken a bit from her, but her blood was strong now—potent: the blood of himself, of Marius and Tavin. He wondered for a mere moment if it was dangerous for her to consume so—but did it matter? If she did not survive it now, could they not just find another like her as they had before? She had quickened them and no ill would come to them from this. Truly, they had no use for her anymore, and being a new Vampyre, she had no idea how any of his feeding on her might affect her. He reflected on this thought and bit into her wrist as she still drank. She gave a light gasp, the blood going through them like white-hot fire, sweeter than wine; a steady, waving hum cycling through and reaching to every last nerve in them both.

Elena was the first to let go, her head falling against Nicolas's smooth chest, but he kept on. So very full was she. So very, very full—

Nicolas finally gave pause, the vibrancy of his being pulsating so intensely that Elena could feel it. She lay, weakened somewhat in his arms, his heart beating hard next to her lips. He stroked her hair back from her face adoringly, her closed eyes opening slightly at the sound of her name.

"Elena—my beauty—" Nicolas's own perfectly beautiful face looked down on her. "I have exhausted you, I see." Indeed, she could hardly keep her eyes open. "Come. Let me give you back some of your strength—"

He opened his own wrist and let his blood fall upon her lips, allowing her drink but stopping the flow himself after so small of an amount had been consumed.

"Come now—" And he stood with her in his arms. "Now it is time for sleep."

He carried her through a panel in the wall, through dark corridors and to a plain stone chamber where his casket awaited. He moved the lid enough to climb in, her weary figure stretching out atop of his and he closed them into darkness. It did not take long before he decided that he rather liked the feel of her there.

Perhaps she could not be replaced, he reflected then. He knew not what Marius had planned for her, but until then Nicolas thought, wrapping his arms around her sleeping body, until Marius stated what would be her fate: Elena would belong to Nicolas.

## Chapter Three

Day broke, but heavy clouds remained and storm threatened. He knew that this mere castle—countries away from where he had been only a few days before—was the right one—it had to be, for the gratuitousness of it gave it away for a hiding place. It towered in the sky and it was surrounded by water with only a bridge connecting it to land. A great expanse of lawn encircled by forest met the bridge at its edge. It was all so quiet here as William stood at the tall, iron gate, nothing stirring and no signs of life evident from where he was. But it was without a doubt, that he knew: Elena was somewhere inside.

He paced back and forth in front of the gate, wondering how to get into the fortress. Certainly reaching the inside would be easy, but getting back out and with Elena was where the true challenge lay. He knew it was already too late—they had bitten her and he had no doubts that she had been turned. Whether or not she still existed—she *must*, he caught himself thinking. He could not be thinking she had not survived.

No, William decided. And they would not have disposed of Elena. Not so soon, and not on purpose. Marius seemed to have gone through so much trouble to get her. For this, William would not be able to remove her during the daylight hours, and at night—it would be such a risk for them both.

He sighed to himself, at a loss for what to do next. The moon had begun to wane and for that he could not rely on the beast he carried inside. If he were to get to her, it would be as he now was, or he would have to wait through another cycle, and that length of time could endanger her further. He would have to find some way and surely Marius would have to bring Elena out to feed soon.

Yes, he decided. That was when it would happen. And when that moment came, William would be waiting for them.

# Chapter Four

Night returned, bringing Marius from his slumber. He rose from his coffin with Elena instantly on his mind, and thoughts of her took him to the vault beneath the fortress where he would find her resting place. He opened the lid of her casket and his heart skipped at finding the rosy satin neat and cold. He wondered—had she arisen early? Had he overslept?

*Had she even made it from the bed?*

He hurried up to the bedchamber where she had quickened them, this thought replacing those he had just had of something akin to happiness at seeing her again, and filling his mind instead with raw dread. But when he reached it, he found it empty as well, and then in a frantic rush, he made for Nicolas's chamber in the depths of the fortress: the only other place he could think of and now uncomfortably hoped her to be.

As Marius was searching, Nicolas pushed aside the lid of his casket, Elena still with him. He kissed her forehead, though she gave nearly no response, and at that moment, Marius appeared over them, shoving the coffin's lid quite off.

"Was that necessary?" Nicolas asked smugly.

"*Nicolas!*" Marius's rage amplified at seeing the frail Elena in his arms. "*What have you done?*"

Nicolas sat up, still embracing her, but seeing as Marius did that her new wounds had not fully healed, as they should have. A little pang of fear struck him, but he quickly blocked it from his mind where Marius would not detect it.

"So we over-indulged a little," he excused lightly as Marius tipped her face up. Elena's lips were tinged with blue and her breaths were shallow, but still they were even and not labored. He turned angry eyes on Nicolas, but the younger Vampyre spoke defensively.

"She is mine, Marius—I made her!"

"We *all* made her—" It struck Marius with disbelief that Nicolas would state such a claim.

"Yes, but she tasted *my* blood first."

"She quickened us all, Nicolas! And she also took my bite first. So you see—it does *not* work that way!"

"No?" He climbed out of the coffin, laying Elena into it alone. "And afterwards?"

"I told you to *wait*! And now look at her—" And Marius looked again at Elena while Nicolas refused to, she still laying there unconscious.

"She just needs to hunt."

"Like that?" Marius argued. "She cannot even leave this vault in that way! And William is out there looking for her, waiting! Do you want her to go to him? After all it took for us to get her?"

"How do you know?" Nicolas challenged. Marius stepped up to him, his ire overtaking all of his senses until he felt he could scarcely see, or hear anymore.

"*Would not* you *be*?"

Nicolas pushed past Marius without another word and left him alone with Elena. Marius looked in on her as she slept—peacefully? Or not? He sighed and touched her face, her skin still burning from the heat of Nicolas's quickened blood. Elena made no movement at his touch.

"So help us all, has Nicolas ruined you."

Another sigh and he turned away, wondering how to proceed, but the sound of Elena turning on the black satin caused him to face the coffin again. Her slender and searching hand grasped the top edge of the box and after a weak moment, she managed to pull herself up. Her head lifted, her very alive eyes finding Marius, his full of relief.

"Where is my lord?"

"We are all your lords—Nicolas, Tavin *and* I." She accepted his answer with a slight nod, as Marius returned to her side and cupped her face in his hands.

"Is it time to awaken?"

He whispered to her, "Yes."

Tavin joined them in the room then, a dark red gown of velvet across his arms. He quickly noticed Elena's weakened state and looked to Marius without saying a word.

"It may be a short night," Marius said to him while helping Elena to rise. Without protest and oblivious to her former modesty, she let the sheer gown she wore fall to her feet. Tavin helped with getting the new one on over her head and he laced it down the back. Marius caressed her cheek again then, a little more relieved that as she moved, she was beginning to look less weary.

"Do not worry, my dear," he began. "Your strength will return and you will be as you should. I will take you out on this—your first night, and we shall remain near for all nights until you have become strong. Come—"

Elena let Marius link his arm with hers and they went up to one of the bedchambers to finish her preparations. She sat in silence as Marius gently drew a brush through her hair and explained to her of the hunt, of the effects of dining on human blood, and what precautions she would have to take to steer clear of harm. Elena tried to focus and remember all that he told her, but her thoughts were scattered and hazy and she felt caught up in a constant dream.

As she stood for Marius to wrap a heavy, ebony velvet cloak around her, Nicolas entered, not looking at all ready to be leaving the fortress.

"Shall you be joining us?" Tavin addressed him.

"No." Simply answered, his eyes locking with Elena's. "I have already fed tonight."

Elena had been struggling to pull from the fog she was lost in, but upon seeing Nicolas, she felt drawn in all over again. Marius noticed and stepped in between them, cutting the gaze.

"I shall wait for you here," Nicolas said to her, taking a step around Marius to steal Elena's stare again.

"Let us get to this." Marius's anger—or was it envy? fired up in him at Nicolas's brazenness. He took Elena's hand and pulled her out to their awaiting carriage, hurrying her inside of it. Tavin joined in their wake and the footman shut the carriage door, before alerting the driver to proceed.

They rode in silence for a time, Elena unaware that Marius heard the questions in her head, though she did not speak them.

"We are going to the home of a very rich lord," Marius offered. "He is an old friend of mine, from long ago. The occasion is a birthday gathering for one of his nephews."

"And it is there that we shall hunt?" Elena asked plainly. "So openly, with so many others around?" Marius smiled at what he took as her eagerness.

"That will come in time."

They soon arrived to the grand estate house, its exterior of gray stone being just the same as the fortress, but a brighter and more inviting façade in its Renaissance Revival style. The windows held curtains, all pulled wide to let the glowing light of the candles and lamps out from within.

Marius helped Elena down from the carriage, Tavin walking just behind them, and the three Vampyres followed on the heels of the other elegantly dressed guests. An unturned servant greeted them at the door, took their cloaks and escorted them to a ballroom decorated in Baroque gold and maroon. Attendees were already lost to the hypnotically beautiful music in a sea of velvet and satin and creamy lace, their dance stealing their feet from the black and white diamond marbled floor. Marius paused, looked about at the montage of those who were strangers only to Elena, and when he found who he was looking for, he nodded and led Elena to their host.

"Come, he is there—"

"Well, Marius," the hospitable Vampyre began, "So glad you could join us." His eyes went immediately to Elena. "She must be the one you have spoken so highly of. The one we have all so eagerly awaited. I am Rigel," he introduced to her.

"Yes. Rigel." Marius pulled her in front of him, placing her hand in the Ancient's. "This is our Elena."

The piercing black of his eyes made Elena's legs go weak and she took a half step closer to Marius. Rigel made no notice of it and followed—her hand still held, to touch her face.

"Hm—" He smiled. "Still fresh."

"Yes. Our stay will be short, I fear," Marius added.

"Oh?" And Nicolas's face flashed through Marius's mind clearly enough for Rigel to see it. "Yes. And where is Nicolas this night?"

"Already fed."

"Ah. Well, then—" He smiled at Elena again and motioned for them to follow him, her hand not yet given up from his.

They went out onto the veranda, and into one of the many large gardens where others sat and wandered. Great, silent interest was taken in the newcomers, and most especially in Elena as they passed. Rigel stopped them at a row of tall hedges bordering the garden and away from the manor. It was dark here, but Elena's eyes adjusted quickly and she noted that Tavin had not followed.

"I know this first time will seem far from what it should—" Rigel began. "A *hunt*. It is actually *quite* far from

28

such an event, but my dear, seeing as you are—in your delicate state, it should—your first—be an easier time."

He put her before him, gently pushing her closer to the hedge, before reaching over her shoulder to part the leaves to let her peer through. In a small, fountained courtyard, there sat a young man in a pale blue waistcoat, light colored riding trousers and tall black boots that shone even in the dark. His unfashionably long golden hair was pulled back at his nape with a blue ribbon and it fell over his shoulder as he trailed his hand through the fountain's water dreamily. But he held a mischievous look in his eyes and an impish curve to his lips, all entailing what he was awaiting. Elena wanted to ask who he was, but Rigel answered before she could speak.

"He is a young aristocrat, notorious for his lust of debauching the beautiful young ladies of the court, and rendering them worthless as brides. It comes to make their fathers quite irate, you see, but it does not sway his interest in the least. He does not care of virtue, or of its value on a dowry. If it is his pleasure to take a maidenhead, he will do it with no care of consequence to the girl."

"Why does he wait there?"

"Why, he waits for you, my dear lady," Rigel explained. "I made certain that his invitation included the promise of some such decadent treat, did he choose to show. I see that it was the proper bait with which to lure him."

"Me?" Rigel raised his brows in amusement at Elena's naïve surprise and he smiled more so when she added, "You lied to him."

"We are already damned, dearest Elena. What will happen to him this night far surpasses being lied to. But he shall not know, nor will he care as it is happening—so enamored of you will he be at his first glimpse of you."

Elena's eyes went back to the figure at the fountain and Rigel straightened.

"Well Marius, Elena. I shall leave you to it."

And after placing a kiss onto the back of Elena's hand, Rigel left them alone. Marius stepped up close behind Elena in the other Vampyre's place, his hands on her shoulders. He spoke after a long moment of their watching of the awaiting lord.

"You see as he sits and waits for you?" he said softly.

"For me—" she whispered.

"He knows you are coming, but not that you are who you are. See there, as he looks into the water? He imagines what your face will look like, what you might say—how your skin will feel under his touch."

The young lord looked up at the stars for a moment then, before lying back at the fountain's edge.

"He worries for a moment that you will not come— but then his brow unfurls and you see his smile? He knows that you will come to him, for no lady has ever refused his company—they do not dare and did they want to dare, they would not know how."

Elena watched the man's movements, his expressions, and every breath precisely as Marius had described, exactly as it happened. And then the lord closed his eyes.

"He imagines you now before him, beautiful and warm and eager, and it brings his flesh alive, his blood to boil. And the things he imagines doing to you—see how his blood rushes through his veins—calling to you—"

And Elena could feel her breaths quicken and she took a step forward, Marius's arms closing tightly around her to keep her close to him.

"You feel it awakening in you—the hunger, the emptiness that you must fill," he whispered against her ear as she strained against his hold. "It grows and it consumes you and burns a hollowness through your entire being. You want to know the feel of his flesh, Elena, like you have never felt such a thing before. And you want to know the taste of his blood, so hot and so alive—"

"Yes—"

"You feel that you will not be able to live for a single breath longer, do you not taste the life that is coursing through him this very moment—"

"Yes, *yes*, Marius!" she breathed, her body living, dying, aching, wanting and she began seeing the trails of red and blue under the lord's skin as though they were glowing streams of light.

"Your perfect little fangs yearn to pierce, to tear and set free the flow that you now crave—"

"Yes, Marius, *please!*" she cried softly, struggling now against his embrace, for every word he spoke was the truth and it had her trembling within his arms. "*Let me go—!*"

"Think only of what you need, take only to the moment I told you of—remember that there is more to be had—" And he felt her shaking turn to frenzied shivers that even he could scarcely hold back. "Now go to him—"

Marius released her and for a moment, Elena remained frozen, catching her breath. But then she was running to him, her sudden bursting into the garden bringing the young aristocrat to sit up and she stopped a few feet away from him, dizzy with her thirst.

"Well now," he began, a smile spreading across his face as his brightened eyes traveled up and down the length of her. They returned to hers and he held his hand out to Elena as she remained in her pause.

"What are you waiting for?" he asked, and it was enough to send her rushing to him, his arms catching her. Elena breathed him in—hot, fresh, the spice of rum—she could smell the life beating through him. She dipped her head to his neck, her fangs throbbing with the need to pierce through his skin, but his hands captured her face roughly, before he kissed her hard and pulled her onto him. She felt him groan as she pulled her mouth from his and trailed it down his throat with novice control. She still shook—he took it as virgin's anxiety and reveled in it—but all she knew was the hunger that had enraptured her and the deafening sound of the man's pulse in her ears. It was as it should be, and through the red-hot fog she was caught in, she knew it was right. There was nothing but Elena and this lord and her teeth found their way to melt into him, setting free the steady rush of her continuing damnation to spill over her lips. She gasped at how quickly it came, choking, coughing, having to resink her fangs as her bite had been too gentle and he struggled free beneath her, while trying to push her away. They landed on the ground, but Elena held on tightly this time, the blood touching on her tongue as it flowed down—nothing before ever having tasted so lovely—and it cooled the fire in her with its warmth, and very soon the man ceased to struggle.

It was then that a chilled clarity filled her head, like the clearing away of cobwebs, and Elena pulled away from him in time for his last breath and the last beating of his heart. And the blood—everywhere it had covered, of her, of him—of a once living person that she had just murdered.

It was a fast-hitting guilt over the deed she had just done. A life taken, and why—? To prolong her own? No. She was already dead! She had been—and now? Now she was nightmarishly *too* awake.

Elena began to tremble again but this time of devastating remorse and Marius reached her just as a painful wailing cry tore out of her. He drew her in against him, her cries lost in her hands as they covered her face.

"Shh—" was all he could manage to say to her. But then Tavin was there, crouching at their sides and Marius found his voice again. "Get her back and do not leave her side until I am there."

Elena quieted some, for the blood was working quickly to soothe her from within. She let Tavin wrap her in her cloak before he took her close, and they went off to their carriage.

Marius remained in the garden, standing and facing the surrounding woods before he began to pace beside the fountain, knowing he and the now deceased lord were not the only ones there.

"It was not how I had wished for her first feeding to be. *William*."

And William stepped into view, his angry displeasure plainly displayed on his face.

"She should not have had to go through it at all!"

Marius stopped pacing and turned to his opposer.

"Would you rather we had killed her, William?" he challenged. William looked away. "I know that like us, you have been watching for her. You must want her to still be present, else I suspect you would have tried killing her yourself when you had the chance." And William's eyes went back to Marius.

"I only wanted her safe!"

"She *is* safe now," Marius argued.

"Are you so sure about that?" It was a biting, growling retort. And truthfully, Marius was also skeptical, but the reason for it was unnamed.

"As I thought. Now, if you do not mind," William continued. "I must go make certain she gets back unharmed, and I shall leave you to—" A nod to the bloody unfortunate.

Marius made no objections to this. And truly, how could he? Once he was alone, he moved the body into the hedging where it would not be found until it was time. He then went to seek out his host, never minding the blood Elena had smeared all over the midnight blue of his blouse, for her anguish was also his.

"Ah, Marius!" Rigel greeted as Marius reentered the house, and Rigel took him aside. "Where is our friend? Our beautiful Elena?"

"She has—" and after a brief pause, "—gone home. She sends her regards."

"I see." Marius nodded as Rigel understood. "And now you shall be going as well?" Rigel deduced.

"Regretfully, I must get back".

"So quickly? But you have not yet even fed, my friend," Rigel stated, knowing Marius had had no part of the gore soaked into his clothing. And this was unfortunate truth.

"A necessity I shall remedy on the way back."

"Please, I do insist. Stay a bit longer, Marius. Enjoy yourself. Tavin has seen to her, has he not?"

"Mm." At least Marius trusted that he had.

"Then she shall be fine." And Rigel linked arms with Marius to lead him into the crowded ballroom. It was on his mind to tell Rigel about William, but he was not certain that it would be wise. Rigel was scarcely a few centuries older than Marius, and possibly a bit more knowledgeable of William's kind. But he was old-fashioned, and Marius mused with wonder if the ironic term could even be used. Marius decided against the asking, for he knew already what Rigel would say of it anyway: keep the Lycan as far from Elena as possible.

"This room is full of thoughts," Rigel began. "Mortal and immortal alike—" He faced Marius then. "I do hear both, you know."

"It is one of your many gifts, Rigel."

"Yes. And your own thoughts are as clear to me as the chandeliers overhead." Marius looked at the sparkling crystals and then around at the guests, trying to keep Rigel out of his head. The older Vampyre leaned close to Marius, his voice hushed.

"Here would not be the place to discuss what is heavy on your mind. Perhaps, never shall we speak of it. But you will know, my friend, when the time comes, what you must do."

A heaviness filled Marius as Rigel spoke, a cold, splintering feeling rushing through him, as it had not for a very long while. So terrible was the sensation, that he could only clearly recall two such times: when he knew he was to be

33

turned, and when he found that he would die without Elena's assistance.

"You are here as my guest," Rigel said aloud as he put his hand on Marius's shoulder. "Do enjoy yourself, Marius, for dawn shall soon be upon us."

# Chapter Five

Tavin lifted Elena down from the carriage and held his arm around her as they moved to the fortress door. Before the doorman could meet them, Nicolas was there, pushing Elena's hood back, brushing his thumb through the drying blood smeared at her chin and putting his nose near the fabric of her dress to inhale the freshly spilt life. Her eyes stayed downcast, and Nicolas indignantly parted her cloak, seeing that the blood soaked the front of her entire bodice as well.

"What happened?"

"She will be alright," Tavin said, slightly famished at her side. Nicolas took notice.

"I will take her, Tavin. Go—finish what you must."

With his own hunger steering him and with every intention of hurrying back, Tavin did not object but nodded, placed a kiss on Elena's brow and returned to the carriage, Marius's instructions lost to him.

Once they were left alone, Nicolas's eyes were back on her.

"Look at me—" he commanded with his silky voice. And Elena's eyes lifted to his. He could see her distress, feel it in her shaking. It made him smile, pleased. "Come, lady."

Nicolas led her into the fortress and into the chamber they had shared the night before. He took her cloak, draping it over a chair and drew her to a basin on a black wrot-iron stand. Without words, he dipped a soft white cloth into water began to cleanse the blood from her face, and from where it had run to her neck. His hand paused as he saw her looking at his lips, her eyes mesmerized by the faint white flash of his fangs. It made him grin and she stepped up closer to him, the front of her pressed to him and her eyes still on his mouth. His smile softened then.

"What do you want?" he asked softly, knowingly. She hesitated and Nicolas bit his lower lip just enough to puncture it and bring a drop of blood to rise. The sweetness of it broke her resistance.

Elena captured his mouth in a kiss, licking the blood in a short pause and then went into the kiss again. Nicolas dropped the cloth and cradled her head instead, breaking away from her mouth enough to bite into her neck to take the blood of the young aristocrat from her. When he had finished, he

35

pulled her up against him and held her tightly in his arms, her bite coming suddenly as she drew the blood back again.

Nicolas gasped and when she paused to breathe, he held her closer still.

"Elena—" he whispered, before he tore through the lacings at her back, leaving her in only a thin shift. He removed his soiled shirt, and swept her up, carrying her to the passageway in the walls. Nicolas took her to her casket, glancing at it before leaving the vault to go to his coffin instead. He set her within it, laying by her side and taking her hand to bite into it, drinking much more slowly this time. So strange it was, tasting mortal blood through her, even after it had passed through him once already. Nicolas did not find it to be as sweet as her own blood, but quite intoxicating just the same.

"My first feeding was a disaster, milord," she whispered sleepily when he had finished. His eyes opened and went to hers, his hand gently pushing tendrils back from her face.

"They do get easier, my sweet. I promise."

"I made such a mess—" she lamented. Nicolas smiled.

"So do we all, our first time. Human blood flows more—freely, than does ours. I do not suppose Marius told you that in his tutelage of you? It is hard to control at first and is sometimes quite—untidy."

"I think I have disappointed Marius."

Nicolas scoffed.

"Have I disappointed you, milord?" she asked cautiously.

"Not at all, my dear. You have done well." He kissed her forehead. "Now sleep. I know it is still night, but tomorrow shall be much different, and you will need the rest."

# Chapter Six

Marius and Rigel had had their exchange of words in the ballroom, and quite suddenly Marius found himself pursuing one of the other guests. The lovely woman had seen him as well, their eyes having locked before she gave an easy chase through the house. It ended quickly in the drawing room near the top floor.

She stood at the far end of the room in her black gown of flowing silk, near the tall, curtainless windows, her back to Marius. He shut the door softly, locking them in and began taking steps toward her as she turned to him. Her hunger—though of a different sort, was quite obvious and her attraction to him clear as well. They were caught in each other's arms, Marius avoiding her kiss and making no hesitation to bite and drink from her, the woman's own desires quickly forgotten, for all he could think about was getting back to Elena. She soon grew limp in his arms, her last lingering breaths sounding as he lifted her from the floor and placed her on the sofa. He wiped his mouth with his handkerchief, the hunger in him fulfilled but insatiably so, for though her blood had been sweet, it had not been like his Elena's.

He could easily picture her face, the new, young Vampyre, and feel her warmth as though she were still in his arms. He wondered how Elena now handled her first kill, and had Tavin gotten her to calm at all? Thoughts of Nicolas hit him then, and they were quickly unsettling. Marius's need to know of her safety and William's questioning words struck suddenly and he hurried downstairs. There was no time to wait for the carriage, fear deepening further at seeing Tavin there again at the manor—without Elena. At the rattling sight, Marius truly hoped Tavin's leaving of Elena in Nicolas's hands was not a grave mistake.

# Chapter Seven

Marius arrived home and burst through the doors, the fortress seeming unnaturally still. He hurried to the bedchamber, seeing it tidy but for the bloodied cloth and Elena's gown and Nicolas's shirt carelessly abandoned on the floor. It took him off then to the library, where he found Nicolas sitting at the desk with his feet on top of it, dressed freshly with a clean blouse, a violin and bow in his hands.

"Where is the daylight, Marius?" Nicolas jested.

"Nicolas! Where is Elena?" he demanded to know.

"She sleeps." He turned one of the pegs on the instrument with smug nonchalance and plucked the string to sound an irritating discord.

"Show her to me."

"She is safe," he insisted. "She is peaceful now, Marius. Let her be."

In a breath, Marius had ripped the violin from Nicolas's hands.

"*Show her to me!*"

Nicolas stood, his mood blackened and he stormed from the room, Marius right behind him. They went to where Nicolas's coffin lay, and within it, Elena.

Marius sighed, relieved and Elena awoke at the sound of him, sitting up and touching his cheek. Marius closed his eyes at her caress, Elena's own meeting Nicolas's from where he stood by the door.

"Are you alright, milord?" Marius reopened his eyes and took her hand.

"Yes. After this night, I only wanted to be certain that you were well."

"Of course." And as Marius could see that she had indeed calmed drastically, Elena could see the true fear in the depths of his eyes. "A few lingering human emotions, Marius?" He smiled.

"The quickening. It brings them back sometimes," he explained softly. She gave a slight nod in understanding, Marius finally nodding as well and giving her a smile.

"Well. I shall leave you to rest then. I am sorry to have disturbed you, my dear."

He straightened and left her, Nicolas coming to her side once Marius was gone. He took her hand and kissed the top of it, all the while his eyes holding hers.

"I shall join you soon, sweet," he promised softly. "Perhaps I shall hunt with you tomorrow night."

And he too left her to her rest.

It was nearly daybreak when Nicolas and Marius made their ways to their caskets, Marius stopping Nicolas just outside of his vault.

"Perhaps, you ought to have her sleep in her own coffin, Nicolas. She shall have to get used to it."

"She chooses to sleep in mine," Nicolas said coldly.

"I do not believe that she is given that choice."

"Good night, Marius."

# Chapter Eight

The day passed with Elena held tightly, cosseted from all in Nicolas's embrace. When night came, he rose with her, but left her to be attended to by the others, and again she was left to the care of Marius and Tavin's for her feeding. She went to the door with Marius to leave, and as far as half way down the steps to the carriage with him. But there, she stopped.

"My dear—?" He retreated back to her.

"I cannot do this again," She could not bring her voice above a whisper, the recollection of her first feeding coming back and she too ashamed to meet his eyes.

"Elena." His hands set firmly on her shoulders, his touch and his voice still with all gentleness. "You *must*. For your own survival. You cannot deny yourself the tending of this need."

Still she hesitated and he raised her face to his.

"It will not be like last night. I promise you."

And she trusted his words enough to let him take her by the arm and she followed, for truly the hunger was again coming on and Elena thought the only thing worse than quenching it was to try to do it on her own. She sat at Marius's side within the carriage just as she had the night before, her arm still hooked through his. Her eyes watched the darkened, blurred view outside of her window, and occasionally she looked to Tavin as he sat across from her. He met her every glance with a warm and securing smile, never being the first to look away.

The carriage stopped in a lively town near the fortress, Tavin getting out first and helping Elena down with Marius following her directly. They both linked arms with her now, and took the sidewalk, passing by closed shops and to the dining establishment at the end of the street. Tavin let go of her and opened the door for them, Marius still at her side. They were seated and brought three chalices of pungent, earthy wine with immediate service. Elena looked at the dark red liquid with no desire for it, and then at Marius, the questioning of it in her eyes.

"Do not drink my dear, but make as if to sip it. It will be believed of you."

Elena did as he instructed, while they watched Tavin leave them to go and speak to a pretty young woman from

41

across the room. Clearly, she was one of the dancers from the pub end of the building, the proof being in her violet, ruffled and corseted wear. It was only moments more before she joined them, both unable to hide that she was a little smitten with Tavin's elegant demeanor, as well as grateful to be accepting the desired absinthe that he had bought for her. She let him pour the water over the cubes of sugar, let him stir it into a milky white and soon after she began to drink it, their lively conversation turned into hushed giggles and whispers into one other's ears. Marius and Elena looked on quietly, Elena's attentions straying with her growing hunger.

It was not much longer before Tavin had convinced the dancer to take a walk with him outside, silently inviting Marius and Elena to join them on his way out. They followed the couple, but at a distance, and Elena began to sense Marius's appetite growing in anticipation and need as well.

"My lord?" Her voice came softly.

"Yes, Elena."

"When will you feed this night?" He smiled and touched her hand as it held his arm.

"Not until after you have, my dear."

She did not ask any more of him, the wake behind Tavin and the woman taking them off of the street and into the threshold of the forest. They disappeared behind the trees and when Marius and Elena joined them moments later, Tavin had the woman frozen with her throat in his hand. There had been no scream, no struggle from her—her lip paint was smeared and mirrored on Tavin's mouth, foretelling that a deceitful kiss had preceded her capture. And now her softly blinking eyes gave no indication that she was even aware of her grave predicament. Elena stopped, pulling against Marius as he had taken another step. Tavin smiled at Elena and nodded.

"Go on—" Marius brought Elena forward. "She waits for you."

Tavin held his free hand out to her and when Elena took it, he drew her near with a steady, gentle pull.

"Her wrist—"

His voice was soft and she felt prompted without hesitation by it. Elena lifted the woman's limp arm, pushing the sleeve of her pelisse up to reveal her soft, unmarred wrist.

"Start there—the flow is not so fierce."

Elena obeyed, her raging hunger intensifying at the first taste of her jasmine perfumed skin, and then the blood came and it filled her with gentle warmth. Tavin's hand touched her shoulder after a few seconds, stopping her.

"Now, here—" And he turned the woman's head so Elena could have her neck. "Small bite at first, to still her," he instructed, though the woman was already quite paralyzed and death sleep was beginning to show in her eyes. Elena did as he said. He stopped her again before she was through and before she was even close to being full.

"Very good," Marius praised, taking Elena in his arms from behind, and Tavin finished the woman off. They left the body there, Tavin and Elena waiting, watching Marius from the shadows next as he lured another victim to them.

The temperate killing lessons went on through the night, Tavin and Marius instructing Elena, and the three of them sharing their prey, until she was sent out at last to capture her own, and deliver the first and near fatal bite. Marius and Tavin looked on as she fed, finishing at just the perfect moment before death set in.

"Ah—" Marius began, lifting her face to him. "Perfect."

But Elena could not help feeling uneasy at the image of her own victim's face, for no matter the hour and no matter that the deed was already done, it refused to leave her mind. He had been young and strong, as had the aristocrat. But this man had seemed proper, he wore a wedding band and smelled of all things good. She had hoped to feel proud of herself for it as Marius did, but Elena felt empty and as lost as she had feigned to be, there seemingly no point in what she had done.

Marius and Tavin finished their night then, the three of them having gotten their fill—Elena overly much, and they reached the fortress in plenty of time before dawn.

Nicolas was not there when they arrived, and Marius could not help feeling a bit relieved for it. He showed Elena to her own resting place, helped her to get within it, and kissed her forehead before closing the casket's lid and leaving her in the darkness. She waited until she suspected Marius to be at rest, before she crept off to Nicolas's casket. It sat empty, beckoning, and she climbed in sleepily to wait for its owner.

It was pressing into morning when Nicolas discovered her there in his bed. He smiled coyly to himself and lay inside with her, Elena's sleeping form molding to his. He had just finished a very satisfying night and yet, he could not resist the warmth coming from her as the new blood pulsed through her veins.

"My beauty—" he whispered.

"*Nicolas*—" whispered back.

"Let me taste of you—"

Without awakening fully, she moved enough to expose her neck to him and he nuzzled it for a moment before the bite. He took nearly half of what she had ingested, a drunken dizziness filling him and a dreamy slumber taking her. It was something he had no doubts about: he could easily get used to it.

# Chapter Nine

Marius and Tavin accompanied Elena as well the following night, but held back in the shadows as she took care of her own needs. Once again, Nicolas did not join them.

"Why does he never come?" Elena asked, as they made their return at the end of the night.

"He has always been a lone hunter," Marius explained. "Since ever I have known him."

She did not question any further on the matter, but could not help but to wonder why he was so accepting of her sharing of his casket, and yet he did not seem much to otherwise care for her company.

It had been nearly a week for Elena in her new Vampyric state, when she was awakened to the sound of raised voices. Nicolas had already left the coffin, and though she could not hear it clearly, she felt one of the voices to belong to him. She had no doubt that Marius's was the other. Elena remained in the safety of the casket with the lid open, trying to listen but making no sense of it all, and she sat up when Tavin entered the vault not long after. His demeanor was quite somber as he helped her to stand, and she could feel the uneasiness that he silently carried.

"Something is the matter?" she half-asked him. His expression softened at her words and he touched her face.

"Marius will not be able to accompany you tonight."

"I hope it is nothing terribly serious—" Tavin hesitated but kept his smile for her.

"Nothing to concern yourself with, dear one. If you would like an escort—" he began. "I should be pleased to join you." Elena smiled back and lowered her eyes.

"Thank you, my lord. But I think I shall go on my own tonight—it is time I began doing so."

"Very well." He continued to smile softly. "I will be out a little later. Dress as you wish, be sure to be in at a safe hour—" She nodded, already knowing all of this. Tavin's smile turned teasing then. "And though it is Sunday, keep mind to stay away from the churches."

Elena readied herself and left the castle, never once seeing or again hearing Marius or Nicolas. Was her blood not already cold, surely it would have run so. Something was quite amiss she knew, despite any of Tavin's reassurances, and

Elena felt positively with every haunting notion that it had the whole lot to do with her.

She decided to finish off her feeding quickly, and to retire back to the fortress for the remainder of the evening, though an uncomfortable shadow hung over her thoughts on doing so. She no longer had any fears of being out alone, or of the hunt itself. What she did fear was what may be transpiring back in the lair, and certainly she did not want to intercept it.

She found her victims easily that night, despite the overwhelming and constant thoughts of Marius and Nicolas. Elena knew that they must have been thinking of her as well, for them having never for a moment to have left her mind. *Yes*, she fretted—their argument had most definitely been over her.

But there had been another who had been thinking of her each time she was out. One who she felt was very close just then, and was he trying, she did not feel he was keeping too well hidden from her. She turned slowly from her prey— an old woman this time, clearly homeless. It had been a mercy killing, Elena had convinced herself, for it was the only way she could get through it at all without becoming haphazard about it. And then with graceful stealth—an ability that she had recently acquired, and agility that startled even her, she put herself in front of William.

"Why do you follow me?" she asked, before he could get over the suddenness of her being there. She recognized him then as the Lycan and forgetting her own immortality for a moment forced her to take several backing steps. "I-I know that you do," she added, foolishly hoping her words would distract him.

"Do you?"

"I feel you when you are near. And I now know that it is your heart that beats more loudly to me over all else. Like a drumming in my head—constant when I am out of doors and you are close. Why is that? Marius says my mortal feelings should fade with time." William gave a slight nod, wondering of her connection of feelings and her discovery of him, and musing at the nervous rambling she gave.

"Yes. A lot of them will be different for you now."

Elena remained silent for a moment, thinking of the night they had met in the forest. The night of her turning. Anger suddenly welled up in her as she remembered the trap he had led her into, and it overtook the irrational fear she had just had of him. How very convincing he had been—trying to provide some sort of rescuing of her, or so he had claimed—and how miserably he had failed!

"Why did you not protect me? You led me right for them! You swayed me to trust you and yet why did you not stay?" she demanded of him. "Do you not know what they have since done to me because of that?"

"I wanted to." His voice was filled with undeniable sincerity. "But as you are now, I no longer have to fear that I will harm you, being what I am."

His words did nothing to dispel her ire, but she remained, questions swirling unanswered in her head.

"So why then, have you now come? What do you want?" Her voice lowered a bit from the raised sharpness that it had been. "If you are here to try to protect me from them or anyone else—you are far too late for that."

"They claim it was your destiny, but you were not meant to be like *them*," he answered instead. "It was supposed to be different."

"You claim to have known this, but you did not stop them!"

"*I could not*!" William protested. He sighed heavily, wishing he had not raised his voice at her, but the entire occurrence struck him with stabbing guilt. "They might have killed you, had I tried. I could not risk that."

"And had they not?" she challenged. "If you had gotten me away from them—would you then have made me like yourself?"

"I might have accidentally killed you instead, no matter what I would have wanted to do." He sighed, his mood very darkened. "I should not even be as I am."

Elena said nothing to that and remained where she stood, William hesitating and then he approached her slowly, holding his breath that she would not retreat further. He reached out to touch a soft dark curl next to her face and then touched her cheek for a moment when she stayed, giving her a half smile.

"Are you not afraid of me now?" he asked, when she did not move and their eyes met.

"You said yourself I have no reason to be."

William smiled fully then and shook his head.

"No."

Elena remained silent, William's hand staying another moment more before it reluctantly dropped. Elena's eyes never left his and he was the first to look away, the intensity of it just too much at that moment. The lack of his gaze made something within her feel weak.

"How did it happen to you?" she wanted to know. "How did you become—like you?" William's smile faded and he began to pace a few feet away from her. After giving it some thought, he spoke.

"A Lycan's turning is quite different than a Vampyre's, in that we are born into it alone. Some think we travel in packs, like wolves, and the very opposite is true. But then, Vampyres are supposed to be damned to eternal loneliness and solitude, and yet they dwell as covenants in large castles. They never reside alone." He stopped, and Elena waited for him to go on. "So, I was riding on horseback through the forests of the north. My father had taken ill and I was in search of the closest doctor I could find. The quest required I take this ride alone, and for the urgency of it—in the depths of night. I could not wait until morn, when it would have been much safer. There was a full moon that night, you see. And there had been—*unexplained* disappearances occurring during those times of the month for as long as I could remember, and for all of my life, warnings had been abound. But, I loved my father and the risk was therefore unavoidable." Again, he paused before going on, though his pacing ceased as he was deep in thought.

"I had not even heard so much as a growl before it was on me." William stopped.

"But you escaped, alive," Elena said to interrupt the bleak silence.

"Alive, or reborn, as it were. Into the creature that I am now. Or at least, what I become when Luna is at her fullest."

"Could you have killed *them* that night?" Elena asked, referring to her own makers.

"If there had been only one—perhaps."

"You *could* then, kill me." She did not ask, but stated factually.

"Not likely." He smiled again and the half-shielded adoration in his eyes drew a small smile from Elena as well. William had no intentions of ever harming her, and this she perceived without him even saying so.

48

"So," she began, as she approached him this time. "Do you plan to always lurk in the shadows of night when I come out to hunt?"

"I hope to try," was his serious response. "Except for the one night each month when it would not be so wise to." She gave him a questioning look and he had to smile again. "It is not a pretty sight."

"You were there, the night I killed my first," she stated knowingly.

"Yes, Elena."

"And was it so very pretty a sight, William?" His smile turned sympathetic and his fingers went back to her cheek in a light caress.

"No," he nearly whispered. "It was not."

Their eyes caught again, something sparking between them. *An emotion that with time would change*—? Elena looked away quickly and backed up a step, just beyond his reach and half turning away.

"I have to get back."

"You think you are so closely watched by them?" William asked.

"I do not know. But when I left earlier, the house was not at peace."

William nodded in understanding.

"I shall follow at a distance and see you safely there."

Elena gave no protest, nodded in farewell and afforded him a last glance before she hurried off. Indeed, William followed, though she was much faster than he, and his heart grew heavy as he saw her enter the castle from the gate. It certainly was not at peace inside of those massive walls.

Even he could sense that.

# Chapter Ten

When Elena entered the castle, her mind was awhirl with questions. She made to seek out Marius at once, and was a little surprised to find him in the library with Nicolas, neither of them speaking and no heated nor negative words seeming to have preceded her entry to the room. Instead, they both looked up at her, Nicolas smiling from his place by the window and Marius standing from behind the desk, his face showing that he knew her thoughts even before she could speak them.

"Why did you choose me?" she demanded to know, darting across the room to Marius. He seemed prepared for hearing the inquiry, but not to answer it.

"You were chosen because we knew you could survive the quickening."

"*How*? How did you know that—how *would* you know that, when all I have heard was that it was not absolute?"

"It was in your blood. In your ancestors' blood. We have known for a long time—we have watched your family for a long time."

"My family—?" Elena began to feel something akin to the turning of her stomach, her mind humming though she fought hard to concentrate on Marius's responses.

"Every so many generations, members of your bloodline have turned."

"*Like us*?" The words disgusted her.

"Yes. But none have survived it for long—usually not past the first night or the first feeding, and none of them were capable of quickening. We lost a great number of our own for that. Still, we thought that they could, but none of them had the strength that you possess."

"So you truly did not know with me?"

"We knew."

"And my father? My uncles—my brother?"

"They would have come looking for you, seeking vengeance. They were not blind to your destiny. It is why you were sent away for the sake of your *education*."

"Could it have spared their lives, I would have come to this willingly! I could have kept them away! You did not have to slaughter them!"

Nicolas had approached and embraced Elena from behind, his words coming softly by her ear and his closeness made her cringe.

"We needed you. The gift you have given us is greater than you could know. You will grow to realize this—"

Elena tore out of his hold, surprised by her own strength.

"It will never be a gift to *me*! But a *curse*—you have cursed me with your damnable gift!"

She fled from the room and headed for the vault that held her own coffin. She reached it and flung open the lid, fully intending to climb in and shut herself away from everyone and everything else. But at the sight of the elegant pink satin that lined the pristine white box, she could not, and Elena knelt beside it instead. She felt that she did not deserve such a beautiful casket. Not for the monster that they had made her into—a thing that was no better than the devilry that had destroyed her kin. She remained sitting on her heels, sobbing even as Nicolas found her.

"A crying Vampyre," he said with a bit of irony, amusement and absolutely no sympathy in his voice.

"If crying is what you would call it," Elena said brokenly. "No tears—" Nicolas crouched beside her to brush his thumbs over her dry cheeks and smiled.

"No tears."

"No—" Her dry eyes met his. "You have taken those from me as well."

"What you are feeling, was lost to me long ago," he admitted. "And there is no going back for it. When I was turned, I hated my maker, until he was destroyed—unfortunate fate of being buried alive by mortals."

"Did you hate him for turning you?"

"I hated him because he deserted me, he did not even bother to show me how to survive and should have left me for dead. I could not even tell you his name."

"How did you know when he was destroyed?"

"News travels fast in our world."

"Then I am no secret either?" It was a proud and then a sad smile that Nicolas gave her.

"No." And then he added, with a bit of jealousy edging his tone, "In fact, you may begin getting requests from more Vampyres for such a precious bequest."

"Of what?"

"To quicken them, of course."

"And must I do this?" That she questioned this brought a pleased and relieved look from Nicolas.

"Of course you may refuse. But the requests, I imagine will be plentiful. Maybe even overwhelming. You may say *yes* just to bring the badgering to an end."

"Will it hurt me to quicken others?"

The slow shaking of his head came, though he wished for this that he did not have to be truthful.

"It will not harm you."

Elena drew the truth from his dark eyes then and he looked down, this slight gesture hitting her with an empowering sensation, her sorrow now long forgotten.

"You do not wish this of me for other Vampyres," she stated and Nicolas's lowered eyes came back to hers, now turned hard as slate stones.

"I do not care what you do—" It was a lie, but what should he care truly what Elena did for other Vampyres? It would not make her theirs and no longer his—*would it*? "But remember your makers, Elena. Without us, you would not exist as you do. You would not have this power."

"Yes. Your *gift* to me," she said rigidly, but then with gentle boldness, she pulled him closer to her with a cold hand at the nape of his neck. "And *you* would not much longer exist as you do, without *me*."

Feeling the threatening of an unstated challenge, Nicolas slowly pulled away, Elena not stopping him, his eyes again meeting hers but this time with questioning of her testing words. He would not be outdone.

"And so it comes to this."

"What do you mean?" Elena asked, releasing him but not letting herself to be swayed by his words.

"It would be best did you not wish to know the answer to that." His voice was low and his hand reached out to cup her chin, his own icy fingers drawing over her smooth skin. "I hope that with your newly acquired wisdom, you will see that it would not be *wise*, Elena, for you start testing to see who is *stronger*." She looked down, moving slightly away from his touch in doing so. This did not please him and he left her abruptly without another word.

"*You cannot hurt me*—" They were words unheard, but she had spoken them, her breath freezing on the air. And at that moment, she hoped that she could also believe them.

# Chapter Eleven

It was her first slumber in her own coffin and she did not prefer it to sharing Nicolas's, but a haunting darkness in Elena's heart warned her that it was safer just then. She would have to awaken before he did and retire after him as well to continue this safety. But fear, she knew, would bring this to be, and there was nothing else she needed to rely on to be sure of it.

And easily, she arose and dressed before anyone else that next evening. Not even Marius was awake when Elena left the fortress only just after dusk. She felt her leaving unannounced was something she was not to be doing, but *masters* or not—what control did they truly have over her? And they could not determine when she left or returned— *could they?*

She clutched her cloak around her body as she hurried on through the gates and along the road thickly surrounded by trees, feeling eyes on her though she did not know how anyone could already be there. And certainly she did not feel *fear*, she reasoned. Why should she?

*I'm already dead*, she reminded herself silently.

Why shouldn't she acquiesce to other Vampyres' desires to be quickened? If it would not hurt but only bring her more strength—why ever not? More strength was not something she held in high regard just then. What she most wanted, and that moment being no exception was to hide away and never to be found again. Or to return home, wherever that once may have been, for at that moment she could not recall it. For most of her natural life she knew she had lived in the remotest area of the mountains, and the sea had not been terribly far away. But now—*now*. Where Marius and Nicolas and Tavin had brought her to, she did not know, could not begin to guess, and she had thus far found no indication of her location. And even if she were to ask someone where she was, she was not certain of how she would get back to her home.

The sudden remembrance of her father and brother passed through her thoughts, bringing her feet to stop under her. Their faces were in her mind, blurry now and she had to close her eyes to see them more clearly. It was useless, the fog over their features growing as dense in her memory as it now grew around her on the road. She could not go back there—what was there even to go back to? Her own people would try to bring about her end now that she was what she was, and she would most likely have to take their lives to continue surviving. The grim reality hit her like a blow to her insides—*she was not going anywhere*—this was her home now and she would never be able to leave.

It was this dismal thought that got her moving again and set her to running at such a pace, that the ground was no longer under them. She seemed to blend right into the fog, becoming part of the breeze and the impersonal dampness as she moved along toward town—a true gift that she knew then she had acquired from Nicolas.

She stood at the edge of the small town, her breaths gently paced and her need having grown considerably. She watched her potential victims as they walked up and down the street, none of them taking notice of her there in the shadows. She wondered how long it would take for them to begin to recognize her, the population seeming small to begin with. No, she reasoned—it would not take long. She certainly did not look as the others did, neither by demeanor nor manner of dress, so very many of them lacking the elegance and grace that carried her. For this, Elena undoubtedly stood out and there was not much she would be able to do to blend in with the others.

She wondered if Rigel would be holding any more gatherings, and whether she would be invited to them, as his festivities seemed a more suitable and perhaps less obvious place for her to be. It led her to wonder of him and how old he was. Certainly much older she felt, than even Marius had said and claimed to be.

"*Years are more simply just a gauge of events at this point—*"

Elena turned her head to glance at Rigel who now stood at her side.

"Are my thoughts no longer secret to anyone anymore?" she asked, not in the slightest startled, though she wondered if she ought to have been.

"To me, and some others—no."

Their eyes returned to passers by, the early evening activities going from the bustle to hurry indoors to the equal rush of those wanting to enjoy the night. The some-steady and some-rushing through of blood in the veins of the living became visible to Elena then. She deduced that it had something to do with Rigel's presence, the same occurrence having happened to her in his gardens nearly a week before with Marius.

"It is something I could pass on to you, my dear—" he offered. She turned to face him at his words, her cloak still held tightly closed around her frame, though more from fleeting modesty for she could no longer feel the cold.

"So. It is begun—?"

He smiled, her conclusion accurate and he suddenly the shy one at the asking. He could not remember the last time he had felt someone else so powerful over him.

"It is something I should like very much," Rigel admitted. "Not only for the sake of being quickened, but—" He paused, reaching out to touch her face, but hesitating to do so. "—by one such as yourself. It would be a great honor."

"I am not certain that I am ready to do so, my lord. Though it is my honor that you ask it of me."

Rigel felt himself swoon at her words. The need for her to quicken him suddenly became very urgent and he grew quite desperate for it, and Elena could feel this emanating from him with each breath.

"My lord, I do not know if I have the strength yet for it—" But she knew as well as he did—she had. She made no more protest, knowing he readily heard her thoughts anyway, and she had no known reason to decline.

"Not here—?" she began.

"My carriage is just there—" And he nodded to an elegant black coach cornered with ebony plumes. And then at her brief hesitation, "It will not take you long. And as you still need to feed this evening, I can easily have that arranged as well."

Elena smiled and with a small sigh, nodded in agreement. He offered his arm and she took it, climbing into the carriage and sitting across from him on a plush black velvet seat.

"Your turning has not been difficult for you to adjust to?" he asked politely, and once they were in motion.

"It feels to have gone rather smoothly, though I have nothing else to compare it to."

He smiled and nodded.

"No. I suppose you do not. But, you are out alone tonight—your hunting goes well for you?"

"Quite." Rigel nodded, satisfied.

"I suppose you know this already, but your makers had long been looking for you."

"Yes. And you knew about this, their search for me?"

"Of course. Marius and I have known one another for a very long time. He told me of your finding years ago, but he needed to wait until the time was right to turn you."

Elena tried to let the rage fill her at the memory of her family having been slain for the sake of all of this, but it did not. She felt quite numb at the thought and did not bother to force the reaction. Rigel sensed her thoughts.

"It was for the greater good, if you believe in such things," he explained. "As blasphemous as it sounds, your existence in our world is nothing short of a miracle. As they needed you, Elena, so do many more of us, if we are to keep our kind *alive*."

Elena's eyes went to the window and at the forest along side of the road they traveled.

"It does not much matter to me, the reason for it all."

"Some day, many centuries from now, when you are where we are, it will, my dear, matter very much to you."

"*Some day*—" But she was not certain she agreed with Rigel on that.

The coach stopped, their journey having seemed lightening fast, and Rigel helped her to step out. The manor stood before them and with his walking stick in one hand, Rigel kept hold of Elena's in the other, and they went in through the doors opened to them.

The house was quiet and few servants were about to tend only to the most necessary of things. At Rigel's nod, one took his coat and walking stick and then handed a lit candelabrum to him. Rigel took it and led Elena up the winding stairs to the second floor.

"Forgive the house for not being as *festive* as it was last you were here," he apologized as they climbed the steps. "But I did not think this an occasion where a crowd would be much wanted—though it is still very much to be celebrated."

"Thank you, my lord." He nodded.

"This way—" he said at the top of the stairs, and he held his arm out for her to step before him. They walked down a long and shadowy open hallway that overlooked the first floor from one side, taking a turn into a closed corridor and Rigel opened the door to a bedchamber, letting Elena enter first. He closed the door behind them and set the candelabra on a table, Elena's eyes going at once to the small figure amidst the white covers on the grand bed gracing the far wall. She felt herself drawn at once to the sleeping child's side, and she pushed the curly strawberry tresses away from a burning fevered cheek.

"If you wish," Rigel began, "I had her brought for you, just in case."

Elena stared down at the beautiful cherub's face, wanting to gather her up in her arms, but the child was so very young and far too innocent.

"I cannot," she protested, closing her eyes against the aching want the girl's sweetness caused.

"Set your guilt aside, my dear," Rigel said softly. "See—?"

He took Elena's hand and placed it on the child's chest, the sound nearly inaudible, but the rough grating of every breath created, taking every effort to make, and Elena could feel it beneath her palm.

"She does not have long to live as it is," he explained. "I know that you would rather her not suffer, as I am aware that many of your victims find peace at your hand."

Elena looked at him then.

"How do you know this?" she whispered.

"It is in your blood and it can be sensed by one such as myself. You are an angel of mercy in your killings, Elena."

Feeling absolved as one so condemned could, Elena did take the child in her arms and swiftly ended her pain, all the while with Rigel watching. It took only a moment, Elena sadly laying the young girl back into the bedding and Rigel taking her attention quickly away with the turning of her head to him in his gentle hand.

"We shall leave now, for dwelling on it will do you no good."

Knowing he was right, Elena rose without another glance spared the child's way and left the room with him. She felt full, but tired and a bit relieved.

"Some never do get used to the killing part of having to feed," Rigel was saying. "I see you are one to which this applies."

"It seems so. Although if I felt I could hate anyone it might be easier."

"You would have to hate a great many people, dearest Elena."

59

They went to the end of the hall and to another stairway, climbing to the third floor, the rooms fewer, but larger than before. The room Rigel took her to was a very large bedchamber—his own, she knew. It was heavy with black and red velvets and flames already raged in the great fireplace. This door he closed as well, and then proceeded to open tall paned doors to a balcony overlooking the gardens. She followed him out to see the grounds below, though the fog had rolled into it as well and nearly only treetops were visible.

"Does it get lonely here?" Rigel laughed softly at her question and looked at her for a long moment.

"At times—quite lonely." He smiled and touched her cheek. "Take your time. I will wait until you are ready." And he went back into the room.

Elena remained for a few moments more, vaguely remembering what quickening Marius, Nicolas and Tavin had been like. It had not been bad—far from it. There had seemed some kind of refreshing ecstasy to it that had made her head and all her senses swirl in a most delightful way. This last thought prompted her into the room, bringing Rigel to rise from the settee in front of the fire, and Elena nearly ran into him with her swift arrival. No words, but Rigel's gentle tug of her cloak strings to release it, his heart pounding with a fierceness he had forgotten. And then the smooth pushing of the tresses from her shoulder to bare her flawless neck, Rigel's ready fangs sinking into it as though there was nothing more perfect in all of the world. She nearly collapsed at the intensity of it and he took her down with him onto the settee, drinking and then catching his breath, waiting for her to recover. It was only moments before Elena, still in his arms, brushed her face against his shoulder, his shirt having been opened and pulled aside for her, and she fed directly from him. His gasp caught in his throat, the power of her drawing blood from him taking his breath away and he felt himself dying all over again, just as he had countless years ago. The moment seemed to last for an eternity, the centuries of thoughts, memories and experiences flooding his mind in the sweetness of the pain.

Elena pulled away after it was done, Rigel's ancient blood having burned like red-hot spice on her tongue, as it now did while coursing through her. It shook her to her very core, the potent one drawing having been quite enough— nearly too much. He grasped her in his arms, holding her tightly until the shaking passed. Rigel spoke first, ending the brief silence.

"Look, now—" he breathed, and Elena lifted her head from his chest to look at him, the glowing red tracks burning through him. He pulled her hand into view and she saw that her blood did the same. Elena felt a laugh bubble up in her at the sight, the effect of quickening Rigel being most intoxicating. He softly laughed as well before taking her head in his hands and kissing her forehead. She smiled and sat up, the renewed Vampyre joining her.

"Will you be alright?" she asked him, this bringing another laugh from him.

"Very much so, dearest Elena. I feel quite rejuvenated." She nodded, seeing the evidence of this in his glow, and she began to rise. "You are welcome to stay longer, does it please you," he invited.

"I thank you, my lord, but I feel that I must go now, and enjoy the rest of the night," she said, smiling. Rigel nodded and retied her cloak for her, before taking her hand to lead her back to the balcony.

"One more thing—" he said. "Come—"

She let him lift her onto the wide marble ledge and she stood there, his hands steadying her.

"Rigel, what—?"

"Just something more I have given to you. And Elena—thank you. I hope you shall soon be returning for another visit." She smiled and gave a nod, wondering why he had her standing up there. "Go now—enjoy your night."

It was the slightest and gentlest push he gave her, right off of the ledge. Elena thought she should panic and no gasp sounded as she dropped, but the cushioning currents of air caught her and she glided gracefully to the ground. Landed on her feet, she turned to face Rigel, seeing him as he still stood on his balcony, smiling down at her. She smiled back and he nodded before she turned away and hurried into the darkness.

# Chapter Twelve

Elena wandered through the woods somewhere between the fortress and Rigel's manor, time feeling to have stood still. It seemed that morning would never come though she was in no hurry to see its arrival, and certainly she was in no mood for sleep. She felt light and nearly floated just above the ground as she strolled, the world all at once alive and dreamy to her. It was so lovely and peaceful and she let it carry her like a gentle, continuous wave. The likeness of it to being drunken led her on carelessly and she barely felt William's presence before she was suddenly leaning against a tree for support and gazing right at him. She sighed, scarcely concerned at his being there this time.

But his eyes were not on her, and did he know of her presence as well, he gave no indication of it. He stood a short distance away, waiting—for her? she wondered. It was on Elena's mind to approach him but before she could budge, she saw stirring in the brush ahead of him. William did not move either, but remained, his eyes also fixed on the movement. Seconds passed and the branches parted and a large black wolf taking cautious steps toward him. Elena held her breath as she watched, hoping that it was not intending him harm, but William did not look concerned and he did not move. The great animal was followed by another and then another, until he was encircled by them, many shining yellow eyes seeing only the man before them. Elena felt she dreamed it all, for their motions were fluid and beautiful, their muscles rippling under their fur and their strength restrained by their own control. She watched as they surrounded him—nearly a dozen now—before they knelt before William and bowed their heads. Still, he said nothing and he did not budge, the painful acceptance of their homage clear in his expression. Together, the wolves stood then, all letting out a howl that gave Elena's heart a jump and made a sob hitch in her throat. It was endearing and tragic, beautiful and heartbreaking to hear. She saw William close his eyes against it and lower his head, as there was nothing more he could do and nothing could change what he was. It was the slightest bit of comfort that shone in his eyes when they reopened, for he knew that he was not completely alone in the world.

The wolves left him then, giving a glancing notice to where Elena stood, still by the tree, for to them she had not been as hidden as she had imagined. At the turning of their heads, William also looked in her direction and the sadness in his face cleared at once. He did not move toward her and they both remained still, Elena being the first to speak.

"What do you want with me?"

"I want nothing with you," he said simply.

"And still, William—you are here." She sighed again and raised her brows with bemusement.

"It would seem that this night you have found me," he pointed out to her. "Though doubtlessly, we would have ended up crossing paths at some point."

"And every night since I have arrived, you have watched me?"

"Yes. Every night."

"Hm. And you want nothing with me," she repeated, unconvinced. "And what of tonight's *unwanting*?"

"You cannot go back there like that," he stated, ignoring her question and his words seeming so far away to her.

"Like what?" She took a teetering step away from the tree, the woods swimming around her then and she realized just what he was speaking of. "Oh—" And certainly she agreed with him, thinking that did Nicolas wish to take advantage of her state, certainly he would be able to just then. "Here—" She held her hand out to him and he came to her then, clasping his fingers around hers, before she took her place on the thick moss under the tree. "For a while. Just, please William—sit with me."

He did just that, her ease at his closeness certainly due to her present state, but it was a relief to him that it was so.

"It was beautiful," she said dreamily of the wolves. "Do they do that often?"

"No," whispered William. "That was a first."

"Oh. They are so lovely—" Her thoughts trailed off without words and her quietness raised William's curiosity.

"Your night has not gone as usual. And I have been slow in catching up with you. What has happened differently this time?" he asked, both concerned and amused.

"A quickening, of an ancient one," she offered a little flippantly and without hesitation in sharing the information. "A sort of Vampyre rebirthing."

"What is that like for you?"

"Mm." She thought on it, trying to collect her words enough to speak them out loud. "Like, breathing flames and feeling it down into your fingertips, but never quite getting burned from it. And—" She paused and closed her eyes, thinking over the sensations. "The swirling of a thousand butterflies in your stomach and then deeper and feeling so very warm and soft and prickling with life—" She stopped and opened her eyes suddenly to look at William. He simply sat watching her as she spoke, nearly feeling what she described radiating off of her.

"Is it always so very wonderful as it sounds?" he asked when she did not say more. "When you take another's blood."

"No. Not always," she admitted. "And only after a quickening is it this way. Usually it is only like a great thirst that does not go away until I—" She hesitated and pondered what word to use.

"I do know that thirst," he said, filling in the pause for her. "It is only so different for me. Just not so often."

"Do you fear your changing when the time comes?"

"Only that I may be in the wrong place when it happens." His smile became soft. "But I have grown quite used to it and so I am able to avoid such disasters."

Elena smiled as well.

"Would you ever go back?" he asked her then. "To being as you were. If it were possible, I mean."

"I know that it was not long ago, but I scarcely remember what it was like," she admitted. "Being mortal. Though what would I now go back to?"

William nodded in understanding.

"Would you go?" she asked him.

"I do not know. There are advantages to this, despite there being complications."

"But you can still see the daylight," she stated. He dropped his head at her words, knowing he was fortunate for that where she no longer was. Never again would she safely see the sun, or walk through a garden to see certain flowers in their full-bloomed state. He wondered if these were things she had thought over already, but then of course she would have. He imagined she had already thought over every possible change she would have to contend with—and probably on the very first night.

"You have grown too quiet." Her voice sweetly interrupted his thoughts. He looked at her again then and smiled, realizing that her hand was still in his and she did not give any indication that she wanted to draw away.

"Lamenting." *For her*, he added to himself. She smiled softly back, still in her altered and terrible comfort, and not seeing the darkened sorrow he felt for her.

"You have so long a time in between your changes," she said then. "Is that strange for you?"

"I have come to know when to expect it, I suppose. And how I am now is so very different from the beast that takes hold—I do prefer being as I am now." He grinned at a new thought. "Though there are moments when I wish I had the strength of *those* times, but all of the time."

"Do you not?"

"Not to that extent, no. If I had to, I could snap a man's neck anytime—" He winked at her. "But I could not burst through a stone wall."

"Can you do that?" Elena asked with surprise. "When you are—changed?"

"No." He grinned again and she did as well at his jest. "I do not think you would be long in that prison of a fortress, could I manage such a feat," came the words with a little somberness to his tone. Through the numbness she was filled with, Elena felt something warm and alive stir within her chest at his confession. It was just the same as each time she met his eyes, but now even more so.

"And where would I go then, William? Have you a fortress strong that you could take me to?" she dared.

Instead of answering, he only smiled once more and began to speak of other things.

"So you have had your fill for the night then? Just from the quickening?"

"I have. Though there was some of that before the quickening was seen to. And what about you? Can you get by on one kill on those nights?"

"I can. But sometimes the beast cannot be controlled. I am most sorry for that and if I truly knew the numbers of those so unfortunate, I do not think I would have much remaining sanity. There is not much I can do for those who get in my way, so I try to stay away from others when the time is near. The few stragglers that happen upon my palate those nights are usually far from where they ought to be. And I hope seldom missed." She nodded in understanding. "Otherwise, it is the other beasts of the forest who get caught up as my prey."

"Do you remember everything that you do, when you are like that?" A dark shadow passed over William's face.

"Nearly every detail."

"I do not like to kill," she said softly. "I am told that it will fade with time, the dislike of it. But I think I shall never grow used to it."

He did not attempt to disagree, though he had gone through something similar and although the discomfort of it remained, something akin to guilt had long ago left him. He did not think it would end up being different for her, though in a way, it was already. His rambling thoughts stopped when she rested her head on his shoulder, though whether she had done it for the purpose of nearness to him or from the spinning in her head, he was not sure. Whichever it was, her closeness made him rouse inside, and he fought the urge to clutch her close in a tight embrace.

"Do you miss the touch of another?" he asked forwardly, not clarifying how and not certain exactly how he had meant it himself.

"I do not realize such a thing until it is happening—" she began, letting her hand come up to rest on his arm, before her thoughts turned to Nicolas and something then unsettling chilled her. She very much hoped he did not come to her that night to take Rigel's blood from her. It sobered her some, the thinking of it and her head lifted again, her hands keeping contact with William.

"Something troubles you?" And William sensed at once that it did.

"No." But it was a lie as she shook her head. He turned to look at her, her eyes peering off into the distance. He touched her face to turn it toward him gently, her skin both cold and burning under his fingertips. She did not draw away, instead letting him see into the jade depths of them. He was not sure what they were showing him, but his eyes were the first to drop, hers turning away slowly with something akin to disappointment.

"You should be getting back soon, should you not?" he asked her then, releasing her hand and pulling away from her to rise to his feet.

"No. I have the rest of the night still."

67

"You do realize that it is almost through?"

His words brought her eyes opened wide to him.

"But it is hours from dawn," she protested.

"My dear, the night is hours long passed—"

She stood suddenly, not having felt the time fleeting away or the morning's quick approach. William smirked at her.

"If this is such the effect of quickening an—*ancient,* you said? I should not think you ought to do it often—"

"I've no sense of the time passed!" She could not hide her panic. "How much longer do I have?"

"Enough. I know some of your kind are able to withstand the first rays of the sun—do you think you can yet?" She scoffed.

"I think not to try finding out!"

"No," he said with a pause and realizing what he had implied. "Of course you should not."

"I—I will get on my way now—" But she hesitated and did not go anywhere.

"What stops you, lady?" he asked with a measure of caution.

"I—I—" She turned to him, and that she was unsure of where exactly she was, shone in her eyes.

"Lost your way, have you?" he teased gently, daring to reach out to slip his hand between her hair and onto the bare skin along her neck and shoulder, and it made her breath catch. But he offered nobly then, "I will walk you there. You've still time to get back on foot."

Humbly and in silence she agreed, but did not accept his offered arm. For no matter that he promised she was safe from him, something was starting in her that was far more frightening than the possibility of harm, and Elena could not bear to touch him just then.

Their short journey continued in that manner, William stopping just outside of the gate with her, his hand lightly on her arm to bring her to pause.

"I do not know in what manner you sleep, Elena, but whatever it is, do be certain that you are alone and that you are safe."

"And what would that matter?" she asked, feeling quite dreary from the exertion the night had taken from her.

He could only offer the shaking of his head.

"Please—the advice of a near stranger. Just, have trust."

"Very well. William." She afforded him a shy smile, suddenly not wanting to let him from her sight, but she knew she had to and so hurried away. She was through the door of the fortress and gone in a breath before the sun could rise.

# Chapter Thirteen

Not seeking the others, Elena went to her coffin on silent feet and climbed into it, wishing there were some way to secure it from within. She had no time to think on it before falling into the most sweet and blissful sleep she'd had since her change.

Only moments later, Nicolas found her there and once having lifted the lid, he greedily picked up her wrist, not waiting for her to awaken before he bit her there. He tasted the ancient's blood in hers at once, the strength of it knocking him back, and Elena's hand fell carelessly against the casket's edge. The motion barely stirred her, but fury sparked in Nicolas at the essence of the blood—not human and very, very old. So she was going to quicken others after all, was she? He was able to get past his jealousy just enough to wonder what had been passed to her from the ancient one and who it had been. He lifted her arm, collected his will and drew from her veins again, having to stop short and not taking nearly what he could have, had it instead been a mortal's blood spilling forth.

He would find out who it had been. She would tell him. If she did not, there would be other ways of finding out. No secrets would she keep from him.

He carelessly tossed her arm down onto her chest, her blood still trickling and wiped his mouth on his sleeve, the liquid fire on his tongue stopping any words that may have come from it. He did not bother to close her in before storming out of her vault to take his own rest.

Elena dreamed a torrent of visions after Nicolas had left her, a mixture of lives and deaths and rebirths and endlessly flowing rivers of blood. But it passed with Elena in its echo, and brought her to immediate awakening as though she had slept for a thousand years and needed sleep no longer. She sat up with apprehension as she found that no one was there, though her lid had been removed, and she felt the ache in her wrist and saw the smearing of dried blood across her pale blue bodice. A vague uneasiness struck her but she felt more powerful than frightened. She would be safe—even Marius would protect her. She knew he would, if she were to need any sort of protection at all.

She found that she was the first in the fortress to awaken, her need to leave for a feeding again taking her to the door without waiting for the others. But as it closed behind her, she knew at once that she could not be the only one awake, only she could not see or feel Nicolas standing so closely behind her.

Elena quickly found herself back to where she had been with William in the early pre-dawning. She happened upon the small clearing easily and knew the way back, the way to Rigel's manor—to anywhere she would have wished to go. It was an odd recollection, but she did not dwell on it, William's presence now as ever there and it pleased her to know it. She waited for him to step into view before speaking to him.

She simply mentioned his name, her smile bright for him.

"Would you mind it?" he began. "If I followed you this night?"

"Don't you always?" was her coy reply.

And "Yes" was his honest admission.

"Would you have me along with you?" she asked as she began walking with him. "When it comes time for you to change?" A bright smile preceded his answer.

"Not if I have anything to say or do about it."

She smiled back but smirked at what she believed was his wanting to shield her from the act.

"Well, then. Perhaps one night, I shall surprise you."

"I hope to God not." The words were sincere, though the pleasant curve never left his lips.

She said nothing more of it, her smile softening as she turned away and set about to look for her prey. William never for a moment let her out of his sight but kept some distance to stay out of her way. He had seen her at it before, numerous times now, but always it was so very bittersweet to watch: her careful choosing of her already ailing victim, the delicate way she stalked, approached and now fed on them once they were within her grasp. And she had now acquired the skill of setting them off into an easeful way, panic and terror being so lost to them, though they were quickly on their ways to their deaths. So very different from the brutality of her very first time, that had seemed but was not so very long ago.

Elena finished her feeding and returned to William, his gentle brushing of a linen handkerchief to her lips almost too endearing to her, and it brought a bashful smile to her lowered face. He felt it, but kept his eyes on her, his hand recoiling slowly.

"Now to where do you go?" he asked.

"Perhaps to Rigel's. It seems to be a safe place for me—"

"What is this of a sudden? A *safe* place? You have fear of harm?" His tone went serious and he wondered if she could sense his pulse as it began to race at the notion, just as he could hear hers.

"Of *what*?" She dared him to say it again, questioning, testing her own fear of it.

"You do not think you are followed?"

"By you," she agreed. "Always by you."

"Not always just by me," he suspected.

"They come along sometimes, I know." Marius and Tavin, she thought to herself. She did not—had not suspected as much of Nicolas, and why should she? His constant refusal of her and the others' invitations for him to join them never changing. Her wrist felt suddenly sore at the thought of him and she rubbed it absently.

"Let us go, if you are coming with me," she said. He nodded and followed her by a step behind. He noticed her nervousness then, her eyes darting across blackened forms, though she tried not at all to let it show.

"Elena—" She stopped with him, feeling her hands trembling slightly now, though certainly it was not from her suspicion of their being watched. "I know when they are around, just as I always know when you are. And they are not—not right now."

"How can you tell it? I cannot hear their hearts like I hear—" She caught herself and paused. "Like yours."

"It is not that for them. It is the blood. The fresh essence of it is overwhelming to me."

Elena tried to calm her heartbeat but his words had got it moving, knowing that he could so acutely smell her as well.

"You have my word that I will tell you if they are near." She nodded at his promise and continued on, finding Rigel's manor and going directly to the door, William staying off out of sight to await her return.

Rigel met Elena in the foyer after his doorman had let her in, his surprise to see her equal with his delight.

"To what do I owe the honor?" he greeted, kissing the tops of both of her hands.

"Just here for your company," she said calmly and though she meant it, there was an edge to her tone.

"You have more unanswered questions—" He could perceive it without her mentioning of it. At her nod, he took her cloak and handed it off to awaiting hands before hooking her arm through his and leading her through the rooms of the great downstairs. They were lit with simple, tall candelabras, all other servants seemingly dismissed for the evening by the deserted feel of the house. The Vampyres took to a long and narrow portrait room. It was empty of furniture, but for a sparse number of overstuffed chairs and a couple of matching settees set widely apart for the purpose of admiring the paintings. Rigel stopped her in front of a grand portrait of a man wearing a purple toga, a wreath of laurel on his head.

"You know him?" he asked her. She found the portrait quite natural looking, the man in it at ease in its setting and the pale sea green of his eyes glowing warmly.

"It is Marius."

"Yes." He took her down to the next one: a man wearing an overly jeweled and medalled Byzantine robe. The gold-adorned clothing looked to Elena to be quite heavy and cumbersome, though it shone like the sun. "And this one?" There was little of him to see but of his face—pale and fine and powerful, with a gentleness to its lines. It was the spark in the eyes caught by a masterful artist's hand that gave the identity away.

"You."

"Me," he agreed. "One more to show you."

Elena crossed the room with Rigel, feeling the eyes of the portrait piercing into her before she even looked into them. A young man with a black velvet doublet, slashed on the sleeves with crimson showing through, both sword and dagger at the ready in his hands. She took a step back, Rigel taking hold of her wrist. He stayed her and pulled her gently back to his side.

"He is not pleasing for you to look at?"

"He lives in that portrait," she breathed, her heart dropping in her chest like a lead weight.

Rigel looked up at it to see of what she meant, knowing the man and knowing how he was in life before he had been turned.

"Nicolas. I am sure he has told you his own tale."

"Only that he was deserted by his maker. Nothing more."

There was a pause before Rigel spoke again, Elena's eyes stuck on the painting though she greatly wanted to pull them away. Rigel released her, stepping behind Elena to put his hands on her shoulders, giving her a sense of protection for her uneasiness. He knew her thoughts, grasped them in a fine string of words before even she could make sense of them.

"He is not one to reckon with. A fierce killer, even before he came to be an immortal."

"What did he do?"

"He was a serf that could not be outdone by hand or sword or wit, and because of this he became a great lord, a vassal to his king—something not likely to ever happen in those times, though this king took him under wing and tutor. He took orders as one of his rank should have, and was promised his freedom should he survive fighting in his king's infamous and outrageous war. Nicolas was of course, victorious. He returned from far away lands to his king with much proof of the win and much treasure, but his king was, as so many of them tend to be—corrupt. Nicolas was stripped of his promising title, his wealth and even his young awaiting bride. He was returned to where he had been found—starving and fighting to live. He vowed to take his revenge, forsaking his loyalty to his majesty. He swore that he would outlive the king and see to his demise himself. His threat only succeeded in getting him thrown into a dungeon to await his own death, which was to come at midnight that same night—for such a treacherous requires no trial for death. And it was then, just hours before he was to die at another man's hand, that he died from a Vampyre's bite."

"And he still carries his vengeance, unsated."

"Yes. Though there are some he will never have his desired power over, he does try to keep what rule he can over others."

"Like me."

"Well, my dear," Rigel smirked. "Not like you."

"It drives him mad, doesn't it? Knowing that he cannot."

Rigel turned her wrist over to give it a glance but said nothing about it.

"So," Rigel began, not answering her and taking her into the next room, this one a small ballroom with a harpsichord in the corner flanked by a row of tall ficas trees. "What are your other questions?"

"Well—" She hesitated and he took note.

"There is nothing you cannot ask, my dear. I may not have your answers, but you need not fear to ask them."

"What do you know of the Lycan that was there the night I was turned?" she did ask then, for her curiosity was too great for her to keep it to herself.

"Ah. Marius knew something of this when you were here for your first feeding. He did not say anything to me then, but I thought it might come up eventually."

"Do you know him? The Lycan."

"We—have never met. But, of his kind, I know only this: there are now no others near here. At one time, perhaps. They have always been viewed as devoted protectors to those to whom they bore loyalties. Some would even say they were kept as slaves, but that was rarely heard of. It is said that when one of them takes a person under their protection, they do not give up the bond easily and it can come to death if that bond is tested. That is all I can truly say of that, and even then it is but hearsay."

"Do you know anything of their turning? What of their relation to our kind?"

"I have never seen one turn, but I have heard that it is excruciating for them—most especially the mortal death they endure, and I would not wish it on my worst enemy. As for their relation to our kind: I know only as it is rumored that their blood does not mix with ours."

"Would it kill one of us, to drink from them?"

"It is not something I know to tell you. They have been too scarce in our population to know much about—as it is, the one you are referring to is only too new to this area. And none of the Vampyres have been willing to take the risk in testing any of these hypotheses."

"Do you think their line is older than ours?"

"You do ask rather difficult questions," he teased. Elena bit her tongue against the others that were forming on it. Rigel sighed then. "Do not give passage for harm to come your way by wanting to know too closely."

Elena's thoughts were circling in her mind, Rigel's words lacking but she knew that the answers were clearly there in them.  They all suddenly went aside when she and Rigel entered the greater ballroom.  It was vast and empty and echoed when Rigel spoke, the light from the waning moon filtering in through the sheers at the windows.  He let her go once they had covered half of the length of the room and went to the veranda doors to open them wide.  He returned to her to take her in his arms, his smile playful.

"You left me too soon last time for us to share a dance, my dear Elena," he stated.  "Would you honor me with one now?"

And though there was no music, there were centuries of it in her memory and in his, and together they found enough of a tune to waltz across the moon-shining floor.  The dance took them around once and brought them back to the opened doors, Rigel brushing stray tresses from Elena's cheek before kissing her forehead.

"Thank you for the dance," she said, having enjoyed it very much.

"The pleasure was mine, my dear."  He kissed her hands again and after a moment's pause he continued.  "I will be having another dance soon—a masquerade, when the moon nearly is full.  Will you come?"

"I promise to."

"Oh, and—if you choose to have your fix here, there will be *guests* for the occasion as well."

The thought made Elena's stomach turn a bit at the prospect of taking a ripe young life, not at all ready for the plucking.

"That is only an extra enticement.  I will not hold you to it."

"I will be here."

"I am pleased.  Now—have you had your questions answered?"

"I think so, yes."  But she had not. Not all of them. Not the ones that were still buried deep within her and even Elena did not know how to ask them.

"Will you not stay for a while longer?" he invited.

"Oh, I fear that I oughtn't."

"You should not worry of *his* jealousy," Rigel warned of Nicolas.  "Your prerogative to know all other Vampyres is yours alone.  He knows this.  He knows it is in your power to quicken all others, no matter his desires on it."

"Yes," she sighed.  "Despite that—"

"Despite it. Know this—no matter the times he drinks from you once you have gained more—*power,* it does not pass to him. He cannot compete with your strength, as it is ever growing. But, I know this of you—and because he is the envious kind, you may not be able to avoid it—you do not believe in bringing about confrontation, and that, sweet Elena, may do you more harm than were you to find yourself in such a way."

"Fair enough."

"Then, my dear, I shall let you be on your way—" He called for the return of her cloak. "I have seen enough Vampyres at war with one another in my time, and many of them suffered quite brutally under their adversaries. I would not wish to see you caught in such a conflict. Most especially as I know your potential enemy."

He tied her cloak around her, holding onto her hands and her eyes with his for a moment before kissing her cheeks and then letting her go.

# Chapter Fourteen

Elena went as far as the gardens where she knew Rigel could no longer see her before she paused to look for William. He did not show and she sighed before smirking.

"Come then, already." For she knew he was there. He did step out slowly from hiding at her words, his head at an ever so slight tilt, and his eyes playfully narrowed at her.

"Had a nice visit, did you?"

"Yes." She began to walk, William now at her side.

"Will you be attending the upcoming ball?" Elena glanced at him, her eyes smiling as she forced a frown to her lips.

"How do you know about that?"

"I had only but to stand across the veranda to hear every word you two exchanged with one another."

"So you heard—?"

"I hear a lot that is otherwise meant to go *unheard*." And he did not say more. She looked away, not doubting that this meant that he had heard her questions about him, and it was to her relief that he did not bring it to the conversation.

"Perhaps I should attend as well," he said instead. "It has been quite some time since I have been to any kind of formal occasion."

"You?" Her eyes were back on him at his playful threat. "At a Vampyres' ball?"

"Why ever not? Do you think that anyone would notice I was not one of you?"

"For certain."

"How, do you think? If I am masked and clothed in costume?"

"Because, simply—you are still alive," she argued.

"Oh, but not entirely human."

"You could pass for someone's breakfast, I suppose—" she teased him then.

The gentle grasping of his hand on her arm stopped her stride.

"An easy enough mistake to avoid," he stated, his tone having gone low as he took in her face, and it made her voice come softly.

"I would know you."

"You would not give me away to the others."

"Wouldn't I?" she dared. His face moved ever closer to hers, their mouths a breath away.

"How, Elena? Would you bite me, there on the ballroom floor—? Would you take a taste of me? Let my blood flow onto your lips for all to see?"

Her breath caught at his words, he so very near and the thought of shedding blood from him stirring her already fulfilled hunger, firing it anew. And with it, something far hotter and even more carnal than the obvious wanting of him.

"I may not wait for that night—" she breathed.

His head tipped up a bit at her admittance, a little surprised that she had uttered the words.

"You still have mortal desires in you," he stated, his own blood and desire already on the brink of a slow boil. She said nothing to this, caught in his eyes and loving the dare he gave of holding on. "Elena, you are nearly still as much human as I."

The observation snapped her from the enticing trance with a flooding of the warnings of others, and she turned despite herself to run from him. But his reflexes were lightening fast, and he caught her in both hands to bring her back and very close to him, no words exchanged but eyes snagging hard and her breaths giving away what she could not hide. He did let go after a moment, seeing much more of what she could not mask before doing so, and she disappeared on the wind.

# Chapter Fifteen

Elena returned to her own coffin early, never speaking a word to her fellow Vampyres, William's stab sticking in her mind like thorn. She hated that he had said the words, hated that he had stuck her with them—hated that they were true. And her hunger that was not for blood—the animal in him knew it burned so very hot in her. And William knew it was for him.

As much as she knew she needed the sleep and though she was closed up tightly in the darkness, when dawn came, she could not find peaceful slumber. Could find none at all. The echoing words from the night made her restless, images of William and the sweet sound of his voice kept her heart racing, and the anticipation of Nicolas coming and the lack of his arrival about drove her mad. She touched the satin that hung above her and rubbed its softness between her fingers. The slick sensation brought more images to flash through her mind—the burning smoothness of Nicolas's skin and then the equally velvety sound of William's voice as though she could see it through the air. The stirring the latter sparked in her and the uneasiness the former drove into her very fingertips, quickly had her clawing at the satin, shredding it while more dry tears drowned her eyes and she nearly choked on them. She knew there was some danger in associating with William—how could there not be? Perhaps she played with the prospect of her own doom with it, but was there not intrigue there of him as well? And Nicolas—one of her makers, one of her own: Who was greater a threat to her? The idea of trusting William, as she wanted to—the darkness that accompanied the thought of trusting Nicolas—she could not take it. She could not continue in this way of not knowing, and more than wanting to be accepted by her own kind, she desperately wanted a closeness with William that nothing else could replace.

Elena suddenly felt as though she were suffocating under her thoughts in that elegant box, and needed terribly to be out of it. It was safe enough to open the coffin in the dark vault and she did so, throwing it up hard, sending the lid flying off of its hinges and it crashed against the stone floor, the top of it cracking in two. Elena sat up, shaking, catching her breath for only a moment and not even fully before climbing out of the coffin and leaving the room on unstable limbs. It was certainly not wise, she knew, as her feet carried her up the steps to the main floor. She knew the drapes would all be pulled closed, safely shutting out the light of day, shunning the rays of the killing sun. And it was indeed so, Elena found, her stumbling steps bringing her into the open hall. She felt weakened and sleepy then—finally, but kept on toward the heavily hung lengths of velvet, something she could not control driving her to it despite what she knew lay on the other side. It seemed forever before she had crossed the sea of the black wood floor to get to it, her luminescent hand reaching for the blue, her thoughts heavy and waving and making no sense. She watched her hand clench the cloth in her long fingers as though it did not belong to her but someone else, the fist readying to yank it back to expose her to her death.

"*No!*"

The word hit with great impact, though it had barely been uttered, and Elena's hand released the drapery, remaining frozen on it. Marius stood behind her then, his hand covering hers to lower it safely away and he stepped around her to see her face as she looked at him. She wore a very lost expression, his one of both terror and bewilderment.

She could only look at him, knowing she recognized his face, but far from recalling him just then. He saw this and raised her hand to his mouth, biting her finger, their eyes still locked. She came fully awake at once at the piercing, gasping at the sharpness, but a heavy weariness remaining.

"Oh, Marius!" she breathed. "What—?"

"Did you know you had come up here? What you were about to do?" he asked. She lowered her gaze, trying to think but could scarcely form her thoughts into words.

"I knew. But I could not stop—" she said woefully. She realized then that had she been but a breath faster than he, they both would have met their end. "Oh, Marius! I am so sorry!"

He sighed and held her afflicted hand tightly as he pressed it to his chest.

"I do not know what brought me here, but that I could no longer take being in my own head," she went on. He thought on her words for a moment and then only gave a nod to them. "Oh," she breathed. "Are you angry, Marius?"

He closed his eyes for a moment, sighing again but not answering.

"How did you know that I had come here?" she asked then. To this he looked at her and finally spoke.

"I do not always sleep like the dead, and I am not— we are not, though I have noticed that you seem to continuously tell yourself that." She wondered if he had been latching onto her thoughts as well. And the slight smile he gave told her that he had. "Though I sleep many thick walls away from you—I could hear your lid hitting the ground. I awaken at every little thing. You have destroyed your coffin, Elena."

"I am sorry," she whispered again and it brought on another sigh from him.

"Where now shall you sleep?" he asked. She only shook her head.

"I do not know."

"Would you lie with Nicolas?" The words came out, even as he was not sure he wanted to be asking it of her.

"Please do not make me do that," she whispered, partially fearing that Nicolas might hear them, and her words were slightly pleasing—a relief, to Marius. "I think him to be quite disenchanted with me."

"I would not force you to," he vowed. "But it might be for the best right now."

He believed those words about as much as she did: not at all.

"Just for this time, Elena," he said softly, his touch gentle, pleading. "Make it the last time."

"Would I not be safer in yours with you?" she dared, afraid of both of her options just then. An odd look crept into Marius's face and he seemed to be reconsidering his advice in exchange for his own desires. Elena was unsure as to whether or not she should have spoken.

"I will go," she said, before he could answer. "But come for me when it is night." He nodded, relief and disappointment both shining in his eyes.

"I will," he promised.

"Do not forget, Marius. The moment it is dusk, come for me—"

"Of course," he whispered.

She turned and took the corridor to where Nicolas slept, lifting the lid of his casket slowly when she came to it, the heaviness of it nothing for her. He lay there, appearing to sleep, his perfect white skin cold and still. Had Elena not known what he was, she would have thought him dead and perfectly preserved. She reached out to touch his face with her fingertips, the feather-lightness of them not stirring him at all. She wondered if he only pretended to sleep, for certainly would he not awaken at the very opening of the coffin? If he had any survival instincts at all—why did he not awaken and demand to know why she was there? She wished Marius had followed along, just to be sure that her little gesture did not go awry. After painful hesitation, Elena stepped into the berth with him, his sleep seeming still deep even when she lay atop of him. She let out a relieved sigh and his eyes opened then, one arm closing around her and the other closing them inside the darkness. She tensed, not knowing what would come next, but had he intended her any ill will, would he not have left them open to other means?

His arms both held her tightly to him.

"Mine again, Elena?"

She blocked her thoughts from him, in case he tried to read them and tipped her head so her neck was exposed to him: her peace offering, he took it as. Nicolas smiled and moved her curls away, taking her invitation. It was, as always, some kind of bliss for them both. A connecting that felt sacred to her though she had shared it with Rigel only just recently. It was not quite the same, however. Perhaps because they shared it so very often. Perhaps because there was more. Whatever it had been, and despite all that Rigel had told her, it now had another sensation coupled with it and she would do whatever she could to keep Nicolas from realizing it: and that was fear.

# Chapter Sixteen

Marius came for Elena just as the sun was setting, helping her to climb out of Nicolas's coffin without waking him. She looked down at him once on her feet, wondering how she had managed it.

"The blood you take—your victims are not well, most often times, no?" Marius asked.

"No. Never." She wondered—for a very brief moment feared—that this would hurt Nicolas.

"It will not affect him much," Marius said, addressing this. "It seems to make him sleep deeply though."

"Yes." And she wondered if it bothered Marius that Nicolas continued to feed from her.

"Leave now, do you want to get your lead on him," he said, without response to her thought. She did not wait for any other instruction and was soon outside and well on her way.

Elena stepped into the forest, hearing the wind as it blew through the drying, turning and crackling leaves. Autumn would be arriving soon, and though it made little matter to her, she could feel a change in the air. It was only nature that made any sort of sounds that night. Elena was relieved to be caught in the middle of it, and for a change she felt completely and safely alone.

Except for William, who never failed to appear. He did not wait for her invitation to show himself, and as she expected that he would be there, she anticipated it. She was unstartled, though her heart began to pound hard in her chest at the very sight of him, and she felt timid this time at meeting his gaze.

"I did not mean to offend you by my words last we met," William was saying with sincerity, once he had reached her. Elena did look at him then, believing it of him. He came closer, still leaving enough space between them for retreat did she choose make it. "It is only that what remains of your human self is so precious. It is not merely a feeling of fast-burning lust to quickly be extinguished or something petty, like greed or vanity. It is the pure desire to feel and let your heart live, Elena, and that is beautiful of you. I admit that it is one of the things that draws me to you."

She remained, only looking at him and taking in his words, the little bit in her that still felt alive, now much more revived than it had been before. She lowered her eyes for a moment and then gave him a sidelong glance and a slight smile.

"I fear that it shall lead me into trouble with you," she admitted.

"And what trouble would that be?" William came closer and lifted her chin with a gentle finger. Her smiled widened, her little fangs showing. William's eyes dropped to them and his own smile grew at the sight of them. He knew he would—and *had* had many similar to hers, many times. But such short work could she make of someone with those four pearlesque blades, and her equally dangerous beauty and charm. He wished he had as much control over his killing moments as she seemed to have with hers, and as much grace as she in attracting her prey.

"Amused?" she asked. He nodded, growing warm when her hand rose and she touched his unshaven cheek, the coldness of her fingers feeling like soft marble. He wondered then if that changed immediately, once she had fed.

"You still need to see to your business," he reminded her and her hand dropped.

"Yes. In time."

"You have something else you must do first, little one?"

Without an answer and giving the slightest pause, she came closer to him, closing the space between them and her cold cheek brushed against his when he lowered his head to her. His arms were hesitant to close around her, though he held them up with a cushion of nothingness between them and her back. Her own hands reached up and rested like mist settling on his shoulders.

The warmth from him was more apparent to her as she stood up against it. She pressed her closed lips to the side of his neck, feeling his pulse beating strongly against them, and it went faster still when she nuzzled her face over it, the slight parting of her lips so she could taste his skin making him draw in his breath. Elena stilled at the soft gasp, smiling now.

"Are you afraid?" she whispered, her mouth nearing his ear. He sighed, deciding that he very much liked the nearness of her.

"No. Not at all," he said softly.

86

Still smiling, she brought her lips trailing back across the roughness of his cheek, down his jaw and to his chin, before touching her lips against his, without pressing.

"Not even a little?" The movement of her mouth to his and the slight frostiness of her sweet breath made him burn inside.

"Temptress—" he breathed, before catching her bottom lip in his teeth, one arm now encircled around her back under her cloak to keep her there and one hand cradling at the back of her head. It was her turn to gasp at the bold move, the tip of her tongue running over his upper lip and he released hers.

"Trouble, indeed," he said softly, his face lowering into the curve of her neck, and he gave many tiny, slowly relished kisses there against the smoothness. "Shall we know when to stop?"

She scarcely even heard the words, shivers and sparks that were most often times vague to her welling up from deep within, and she only tipped her head away to accept more caressing of his lips.

"Perhaps," he whispered against her ear, pausing to lick the edge of it lightly. "You do not want this to stop—"

"Perhaps you are right—" Elena could not tell if she said the words aloud or not, but knew she must have, feeling William's smile against her skin before more kisses replaced it and trailed down into the hollow of her throat. She moaned softly, her head going back in his hand and his kisses lowered daringly further to her already immodest neckline. Her skin did seem to warm under his touch, but cooled instantly the moment he left it free again. A gentle tugging on her dress bared her shoulder and he bit it lightly, not breaking the skin. Elena gasped again, his kind of bite so unlike the ones she had grown used to. It was softer, sensual and as she knew he was not biting to draw blood, it gave promise that there was no telling where it would move to next.

"Elena—" his whispers continued, and she breathed in response.

"William—"

Elena did not stop him, feeling his hands on the laces at her back, his kisses trailing up the other side of her neck. She only moaned in answer, feeling the ties on her bodice lacings spread as the knots came free in his fingers, her own reaching in front of her to pull his buttons free from his shirt.

87

His breaths drew in sharply and quickened when her fingertips slipped in between the fabric and his skin.

"How far are we going to take this?" he asked at her touch and keeping his own head lowered against her neck.

"You have started this fire, William—"

His head lifted suddenly, their eyes meeting so very briefly, and without any explanation, he left her there, the cold filling her like rushing water.

"Elena—"

She turned suddenly at the calling of her name. It was Nicolas who approached her then and she hoped at once that he had not seen William there with her. "This is a strange place for you to try finding your breakfast," he stated. She had no time to answer him before Marius joined them, and she could tell from the look in his eyes that he had seen something. She could only hope that he would say nothing about it, at least not until they were alone.

"To town then?" Marius asked as he took her arm, Nicolas taking the other one before she could say a word to either of them. She knew that Marius would hear every last thought that she might have just then, but it was Nicolas's knowing that she feared.

*Do not let him in* she thought while looking at Marius, her eyes pleading to him.

"I have received our invitations from Rigel. He will be having another party," Marius said, pulling his eyes from hers. He felt her arm tighten on his just slightly in gratefulness, and as his hand set on top of hers, he continued on about other masquerades that his friend had held in the past. So many details did he rattle off, one after the other, that Nicolas at last interrupted him with impatience.

"Will we never feed this night, Marius? Or would you rather continue on with your prattling? I, for one greatly starve, so let us be at it already."

He did not wait for Marius to react before leaving them and hurrying off to find his own victim. Once he was certain that Nicolas was gone, Marius turned to Elena, sharply lifting her lowered face up to his.

"I cannot keep him out of your head all of the time!" he warned. "I also cannot keep him from feeding on you, because he has a *way* about himself with you that I know you do not bother resisting."

"What am I to do, Marius?" she asked, nervously. "Is he not stronger than I? I cannot help but to wonder if it was he who led me to the window this morning. Would he regret the destruction of me? I cannot tell and yet he seemed relieved that it did not happen once I had crawled into his coffin with him."

"He is not stronger than you, Elena," Marius began, hating the image of her lying with Nicolas. "You know this— have been told this. It is *true* and you must believe it. But there is another danger that you are tempting, my dear, and you *cannot*! You must stop this now!"

*William.*

"He is no threat to me," she insisted.

"It is not wise, Elena. *It is not*! When he approaches you, you must leave him. You must stay with your own kind! There are those of us who fear for you of this tampering you tempt, but Nicolas of all, will not stand for your *interactions*. It is not Nicolas's strength that you should fear but does he ever learn of this, he will find a way to punish you! Do not let yourself risk getting caught!"

Elena let out an exasperated sigh and turned from Marius, wondering why Vampyres, of all creatures must have any kind of concerns what so ever.

"I will continue to see him when I am out at night," she said firmly. "Because you cannot stop that and neither can Nicolas. I dare say, not even I can make him stop."

To this Marius only nodded, knowing that it was true.

"I do appreciate what you did a moment ago," she said, giving him a bright smile that even at that moment Marius could not resist softening to. "Is there anything I can do for you?"

It was an improper request he would have for her, he knew. But one that would be asked despite the wrongfulness of it. Elena saw him hesitate and her smile faded.

"What is it, Marius? Ask."

"I have made arrangements for you to have a new coffin," he began. "When it arrives, go to it and sleep only there. Stay out of Nicolas's."

"That is all?" she asked, knowing there must be more as she could see it in the pale green of his eyes.

"I will come to you about it later."

And he left her then as well, Elena thinking over his words. She knew William would not show again that night, whether he was close or not and watching from the shadows. She wondered if he had heard what Marius had said. She hoped not, but was certain that he probably had.

"Elena—" Nicolas called from the edge of the trees.

She went to him, not wanting him to come to her there in the seclusion of the trees, and she found him with fresh blood running through him. He took steps closer to her then.

"Are you not hungry?" he asked. Indeed she was, had been—as she had been so very close to taking a bite earlier of William, before he had distracted her in other ways.

"Yes, I am on my way."

"Do not be long. I will be waiting for you," he promised, the smell of sweet, healthy blood mixed with his words. She sighed, wanting to feed on him instead of finding her own death-sleepy blood to drink, and she dared not let her taste dwell on how lovely a strong victim might be. He felt this from her and grinned. "Perhaps once you have returned, we shall make the exchange," he suggested. She nodded, his fingers cold and soft against her cheek.

"I will be along soon, Nicolas," she promised, her voice a purr against his ear.

"Yes. And do you not make it exactly that—*soon*, I shall believe that someone has stolen you away."

She only smirked, letting it be another Vampyre that came to mind, hoping it would keep Nicolas off of her deeper thoughts.

"Of course," she whispered.

He left her alone then, but she knew he could not be far away. At least, she knew she could not let herself believe that he was. Never did Nicolas come out to hunt with them— why now? The question was unsettling. Did he see something in her mind? In Marius's? He never went to Rigel's that she knew of. She hoped Nicolas did not speak to William at any time, for however would the Lycan keep Nicolas out of his thoughts, or even know that he could see into them?

Elena made her search a quick one, her victim not an ailing one this time, so much as a drunken one, spiraling his way into poverty and certain illness that would lead him into the state of her usual choice. It was a terrible feeding, she decided, but she made it out of the hasty fear of discovery. As well, she returned, going immediately to Nicolas where he awaited her in the study, his violin in hand.

He smiled at her entry, her composure only slightly edged with the evidence of her rush. It brought him to his feet from the chaise where he had lounged with anticipation of her arrival.

"So soon?" he asked, tossing the bow to the desktop and taking her offered wrist in hand, the violin still in the other. He stood behind her then, crossing his arms in front of her, her wrist in open view. Her eyes closed as his face lowered to her neck, her sigh coming at the closeness of him and the exhilarating chill of his teeth on her flesh. He made to bite her there, the gesture turned suddenly, slowly into a gently sucking caress with his lips. Elena felt herself melt back against him, his hand still holding her wrist, raising it, and with the other, he swiftly drew the violin strings across it. She gasped at the sting as six crimson rivers rose up and he let them run for a moment before dropping the instrument onto the chaise. She turned to him, the blood running hot and steaming up from her. He gave one more pleased smile before licking the streaks and then drinking from them, all the while his arm holding her tightly against him. Elena felt her legs give way through the haze growing in her head, falling sleepy in Nicolas's arms. The taken blood made his head hum, more alive than usual but inebriating as it had been for Elena. He stopped himself before he took too much and swept her up into his arms.

"Time for sleep, my lady," he whispered, with no intentions on sharing his blood with her. Elena gave a vague response, too weakened to protest as he carried her to his casket and put her inside. She felt slight movements as he joined her, did not see the lid come down, for her eyes had become leaden and there would be no opening of them until the next nightfall.

# Chapter Seventeen

When Elena awoke the next evening, Nicolas was already gone. She made a search of the fortress and found that Tavin and Marius were also missing. Only one reason came to mind and it struck her in a panic: had they gone looking for William?

She did not know what sort of interactions of the Vampyres to William's kind would be acceptable, nor of their laws did one such as herself cross the line or even attempt to. Like Rigel, she did not know if William was alone in his world or if there were others, and had the Vampyres sent out a search party for him that night, Elena feared that they—was it their determined intentions—would surely find him and end his life without hesitation.

Like on so many other nights, Elena could have found her way to ready herself, to dress the part. But as setting about to search for a victim and feeding were not her greatest concern, she only pulled on a filmy white dressing gown that she would just as soon slumber in, the ends of it lifting and flowing on the gentle wind.

She rushed out of the fortress and into the forest like a ghost, her bare feet scarcely touching the ground as she swiftly moved across it. She made way to all of the places that in the past she had seen William and she found him nowhere. She could not hear his heart as she usually could and Elena dared not call for him, in case anyone else might be about. But as well, there seemed to be no one else around either. She could hear nothing but the wind in the leaves, she could not smell fresh blood as William was able—there was nothing.

Night was not long to be, when Elena gave up her search. She was hungry, tired and full of disappointment. She did not want William to be caught by the others, but selfishly, she wanted so very much to see him and to touch him again that she would have risked it. She knew that it was not fair of her to think in such a way—not fair for William. It was most likely not safe for him and she needed to remember this for his sake.

Elena began to sigh but it turned into a defeated half-cry, such was her extreme discontent. It had been but one day separating this night from the last since she had seen William. Surely there would be many nights where she would have to give up their meeting, she reasoned. Did she handle each one of them in such a way, Elena was certain that she would indeed go mad.

But had he not said before that he was always there with her somewhere? She had believed it when he had told her so, and but for the lack of his heartbeat and the drumming in her head, she would believe it still of that moment. Her heart began to hurt then and Elena felt the return of more emotion, rather than the promised growing lack of it. What was it for? she wondered. The flashing of his sparkling blue eyes through her mind distracted her thoughts. She was never going to survive being separated from him at this rate!

She only wanted a moment with him. Just a singular, tiny little moment of the night and she would be satisfied until the next time. If it was all that she could have, then she would take it.

Elena closed her eyes and took a deep breath, before letting it back out again, wishing, hoping—

And as her eyes remained so, shutting out the world, in a breath his presence came and went, in the brushing of his cheek against hers. Elena gasped and opened her eyes to see that she was alone, and she would not have believed for a second that it had been otherwise, did her cheek not burn where he had touched it with his. Elena's hand went to it, and she closed her eyes again, smiling and feeling warmed into her every nerve.

And then the sound of Nicolas's voice shattered the bliss.

"You are dressed poorly for being out on the prowl," he stated. As Elena opened her eyes once more, the remembrance of needing to feed filled her with a cold and hard ferocity. She did not give him time to react before she turned to him and seized upon his throat, taking her needed nourishment from his veins. Nicolas tried for only a fleeting moment to stop her, but the feel of it was too intense, too pleasurable for him and he could do nothing but hold her in his arms.

The blood was young, post-virginal, but barely and Elena abhorred that Nicolas had most likely interrupted a wedding bed for his dinner. Still, it did not surprise her and she did not feel like stopping herself. He dropped to his knees, Elena still holding on tightly, Nicolas now dizzy and dumb from it. It was not he, but Marius who pulled her away from him.

94

Elena came to her senses once separated from Nicolas's blood, quickly wiping her face onto the pure white of her sleeve for she has been quite careless in the act.

"Get back, Elena," Marius directed. "I will put Nicolas to rest and find you at your bed."

Elena nodded, a bit surprised that he had not met her with a hard reprimand. Her eyes dropped to Nicolas, who sat back on his heels, his face sleepy and showing that he had no wits about him just then. She was startled to see that she had come so close to taking far too much blood from him. She had not realized how very hungry she had been, but as she hurried back to the fortress, she did wonder if perhaps it was not just the need for sustenance that had driven her so, but perhaps it had been in the pursuit of a different sort of survival.

The thoughts left her a bit uneasy as Elena returned inside and through the corridors toward her vault. But was there not a little bit of triumph there as well? She did not want to think of it that way, for no matter how Nicolas was toward her, Elena did not wish ill for him.

And just before that—William. Her hand went to her cheek again and it burned anew. How sweet the contact had been! How so endearing that he had known her thoughts and her wanting of his presence. And much more so precious that he had granted her wish! It was then so very hard to continue on to the vault when all she wanted more than anything was to rush back outside to find him. It was not to be—it could not be—for she knew the sun was coming up shortly and she had to be safely shut inside. It was a fast flashing through her mind, as she wondered what it would be like to sleep in William's arms. She had to stop her thoughts of him while inside the fortress. Had the Vampyres not thought to hunt him down yet, surely her private notions would make it so.

Elena pressed on through the halls, knowing that her new coffin awaited her in its chamber, and despite Marius's instructions, she could not help feeling drawn to Nicolas's own berth. She fought the pull of it, knowing she had promised Marius that she would not again go there. At least this one night? She did not know how long she would be expected to sleep in her casket alone, but she did not have long to ponder it, as Marius followed right on her heels into the room.

"Is it to your liking?" he asked when her eyes set on the coffin.

"Oh—" And she looked at the mahogany box with its intricate vine carvings and deep green velvet interior. "Yes, it is beautiful."

He nodded at her approval, now hesitant on the true explanation for his being there.

"Marius."

"It is my—request—that brings me here to you."

"Yes, what is it?" she asked, wanting to feel free of any obligation to him. Still he hesitated. "Anything—" she added, if only to prompt his answer.

"What you give to Nicolas—I ask that you give it to me, this once, instead."

Her thoughts froze as she tried to comprehend what he was asking. It filled her then with chagrin and he felt it. But if it did not harm her for Nicolas to do it, what harm could there be in allowing Marius?

"Never, will I ask this of you again," he said. "I should not be asking it now—"

And truly she did believe him. It was the only factor that brought her to climb into her coffin and raise her hand to him. For a moment he hesitated, her hand in his and his lips pressed against her skin, his eyes closing just at the feel of her.

"Just—not so deeply," she whispered and he nodded respectfully.

"There is a lock on the inside," he told her then, his eyes opening. "I will leave you enough strength to make use of it. And Elena—" Their eyes met at the uttering of her name, the pleading that sounded in his voice. "Please use it!"

She only nodded and Marius drank from her, just as Nicolas would have had she gone to him that night instead, and had she not beat him to it. She did not feel Marius gasp or hear him fight to catch his breath, so enrapturing had it been for him. Nor did she hear him leave her when he finished, and only scarcely did she feel the lid close on her after Marius had placed the key in her hand, with the words *lock it now* echoing in her head.

Nicolas waited in his casket for Elena for a short while, Marius having revived him just a bit with his own blood. Nicolas knew that she was not coming to him when he began to grow tired again and she had not yet arrived and gave no indication of it. Irritation and anger welled up inside of him and he rose, going at once to where her coffin was kept. The small, new and elegant box sat on its marble pedestal, the lid closed. He went to lift it and found that it was locked for it did not budge. He gave it another try, wanting to shake the casket and push it to the floor, but Marius had made sure to anchor it firmly down, and the lid simply would not give. Nicolas knew Elena was inside of it. She was hiding from him—or hiding something. His fury grew hot and he would be certain to find out why she had not come to him, and why she was evading him now. For tonight, he would give up—for now he could only settle with bringing his fists down hard on top of it, in the hopes that the sound and the motion would awaken her. He hoped that it would frighten her and leave her with uneasy sleep for the night. *How dare she deny him*?

Nicolas stormed off back to his casket and climbed into it, bringing the lid down with a crash. If she decided to show and attempted to join him, he would be certain to shove her right back out. He spent the moments before sleep stewing over her choice of beds. Could he have set fire to her coffin and burned her and it together without taking down the rest of the fortress, he would have. Could he have dragged it outside and left it for the morning to consume, there would have been no stopping him—oh how he would love to see her open it, unaware, only to find that she had been greeted by the dawn! And could he have ripped off the lid and plunged a stake into her heart, he would have done that as well, such was his rage.

Her time would come, Nicolas decided. He would be sure to let her know who was stronger, and forever until the end of her lifetime as a Vampyre, he would remind her to whom she would always answer.

# Chapter Eighteen

Elena awoke with the end of the ribbon that held her key in her hand. She did not feel as tired as she usually did the evenings after Nicolas got to her, and though it left her feeling a bit uneasy at the memory, she was grateful that Marius had respected her request and had not taken so much of her blood. But he had promised that it would only be this one time and never again. Still, she did not wait for him or anyone else before she left for the night-darkened woods and began with the greatest caution to look for William.

It was after long moments of searching and for a moment she recalled his leaving of her two nights before—how abrupt it had been. Certainly it was because Marius and Nicolas had been there. And just the night before—only that gentle and almost dreamlike encounter whose integrity she now wondered of. But now that William was not showing—did that mean that the Vampyres were again near her too? She closed her eyes and sighed with deep disappointment, his once-perplexing presence now suddenly missed more than ever and she knew that just one solitary touch—though it had gotten her through the night before—it was not going to continue being enough. She wondered if she could call to him without speaking, as she seemed to have before—but his hearing was so acute, would he at the very least hear her if she just whispered his name—?

"*William*—"

Before her eyes had the chance to open, he had her around the waist and lifted her from the ground, taking her this time more deeply into the density of the trees. He set her down when he felt it safe to do so, his hands cradling her face.

"I am sorry I left you the way I did," he began, his breathing labored and Elena taking a moment to calm after his surprising of her. "And that I could do no more than I did last night—you understand that it was the only way?"

"Yes, William. Of course."

He smiled at her and kissed her hand, not letting go of it, as her free one met his cheek with a gentle rub.

"My William," she said softly.

"Yes, dear heart."

"What would have happened, had we not been interrupted a few nights past?" Her question was bold, she knew, and before she could stop the words they came out. And this made him grin most rakishly.

"What do you think?" Her eyes met his for seconds and then dropped again, her insides shivering from the intensity of them.

"Are they close again tonight?" Elena gave a cautious look around, while stepping more closely to William.

"Sadly, yes. They do keep such close watch on you at times, and most recently much more so. My time with you tonight will be far too brief."

She sighed and nodded.

"Perhaps another night?" He saw her brow rise mischievously and William smiled, his eyes sparkling.

"Most assuredly."

"And soon?" She inched as close to him as she could, his hand closed against her back, pressing and holding her there.

"Positively soon, Elena."

"What shall happen, if I bite you?" she asked then. He shook his head slowly.

"Sincerely, I do not know."

"It does not terrify you at all?"

"That you would do it?"

"Of what might happen to you, of my venom, if I do it."

"No." His answer surprised her a little.

"Do you wish it of me then?"

"We shall see."

Elena looked into his eyes again, letting herself fall into them and his face grew serious, dreamy. His hand drew up and softly down along side of her face. He saw her lips part as if to say something but she changed her mind and it made his mouth ache to kiss her.

"What is it, Elena?" he whispered.

"William—" she began, feeling the same yearning. Her eyes dropped to his cheek, to his chin as her fingertips ran over the coarse brown hairs, and then paused on his mouth.

"Yes, little one."

"I feel safe when you are near."

Her words struck a sweet chord in him and he took her face in both hands, placing a kiss on top of her head, though he wanted nothing more than to give in to his desires. He knew he could not just then, he had to wait, for there was

100

just not enough time. He sighed instead, before tipping her face up to him.

"I am glad for that. I intend to keep you safe."

"I could get lost in your eyes," she admitted, feeling pulled into them already. He loved the feel of her touch, and smiling from it, he took her hand to press her palm to his cheek again. At this, she lifted her other hand and cradled his face with them both, brushing against the scruff of his beard.

"When the moon is bright," she began, "let me see you. Please, William. I am not afraid."

"No, my love," he said sadly, stroking her hair and clenching the locks in gentle fists. "It is not for you to see."

"Why do you try to hide it from me?"

"It is not the beast I want to shield you from, my dearest. But the destruction it brings."

"It is no worse than what I cause."

"It *is*," William insisted, the horrific gore of it sickening the human side of him just at the thought of it. When she made to protest again, he continued. "You are more than a Vampyre to me, Elena. You are still the sheltered lady that I tried to protect on the night we met. You are still that precious and sweet maiden to me. Please do not ask to see me acting out those evil ways."

"Oh, William!" she sighed, pressing her forehead to his. "You have such a pure heart! I suppose you still say your prayers before you sleep?" He smiled at her teasing jest.

"Not so often as I should," he admitted. "But I do try to remember to say them for you."

"There is no saving me now, William,"

"In a manner of speaking, I believe there still is."

Another twinge struck the still-human part of her and the bittersweetness took away her words. Elena dropped her hands from his face and wrapped her arms around his neck, embracing him tightly and William did the same of her waist, lifting Elena's feet from the ground.

"Oh, William! How would this be bearable without you?" Her wondering had her not wanting to let go of him. His arms remained tightly around her.

"I should ask the same of you, my little one." He set her down with great regret, taking her face into his hands again, for he wanted always to be touching her.

"It is time?" Her question afforded her a sad smile.

"I am afraid so. But there is tomorrow night."

"Yes, of course."

"And Elena—just because you do not see me, does not mean that I have left you. I am always near you—always just a breath, just a calling of my name away."

"I know this, my sweet William."

"Good."

Again she made to speak but stopped herself, and William grit his teeth and closed his eyes with a sigh against his wanting of her.

"Go, my sweet," he whispered. Elena stood tall and kissed the corner of his mouth before she rushed away on the wind.

# Chapter Nineteen

Before Elena could climb into her casket, Nicolas was there, his hand crashing down on its lid to stay it.

"So you are deserting me, are you?"

Elena jerked her hands away and stuck them behind her back, and tried not to let her nervousness show at the great displeasure sounding in his voice.

"Marius thinks it is best," she stated, hoping Marius would not mind her putting the blame on him, though she did not think he would contradict it.

"Since when does Marius know best?" Nicolas had asked it of her, though it was more to himself. "It is what *you* want. *Is* that what you want?"

She hesitated, thinking out her answer carefully.

"Last night, I nearly brought you irreparable harm," she forced out. "It is never my intention to hurt you, Nicolas, and I would never want to. Being here will protect you do my desires get out of hand."

He scoffed at her excuse, insulted that she thought she could do him any sort of damage.

"It is more than that," he insisted. "There is something more."

"There is nothing more." Elena fought hard not to think of William, but it was so very challenging to keep him from her thoughts when she wanted to think of nothing else, and Nicolas seemed to be pulling hard from the depths of her mind, drawing her thoughts out as though they were loose threads. "What could there possibly be?"

"Perhaps you want to skip your feedings and come to me for them?" he answered suddenly and taking Elena by surprise. "Perhaps you want to trade roles and have me sleep with you instead of coming to me."

"Perhaps—" she played along. And it was becoming clear to Elena that she wanted nothing of the sort and his eyes suddenly darkened at her.

"Well, you will not get that, sweet thing! Do you enjoy your own coffin so much, Elena, then you should stay in it all alone. Do not dare to come to mine again!"

And Nicolas stormed out, leaving Elena with a pounding heart and an aching head. The pressure of his mind bearing down on hers left as he did, and she wondered how she had been able to shield herself from him and throw him

103

off of her thoughts. She knew then, as Marius stepped out from the dark shadows, his finger rising up to his lips before she could speak. He left her without saying a word.

# Chapter Twenty

Elena took great precautions henceforth, always awake before the others, always in last and sometimes just in the nick of time after. She despised that she had to lurk about with so much caution and take such great care with her whereabouts. Most especially she hated that her meetings with William were made in such miniscule doses, often times resulting in little more than their passing by one another in the woods, their hands meeting, grasping for mere seconds before painfully letting go. And each time, the exchanged glances, the quickly fleeting touches and the anticipation of more resulted in the fierce kindling of the fires growing within them both.

On many occasions, Elena would find him and so very close they would come to one another, so tightly would they embrace, and all too immediately would William have time only to whisper in her ear "*Quickly love—*" before she would have to move on with the wind, her mouth aching for the kiss that never came and his entire everything craving the devouring of her in any way he could.

Elena stood at the window in the library as Marius sat in a chair, pretending to read. Tavin had braved the falling rain to feed with the promise of providing for them all upon his return, and Nicolas sat casually, lazily on the chaise, watching Elena. She did not afford him a glance, trying to think of nothing but the trickling rain drops on the multicolored stained glass, when every few seconds she allowed a fleeting flash of William through her mind. She raised her fingers to rub over a small shape of aquamarine glass, the color of it being exactly as his eyes. She did it often when she was stuck within this room, so much so that Nicolas was prompted this time to mention it.

"I swear you shall take the color right out of the glass, do you continue to do that, Elena."

Her hand dropped at his words as though he had tainted the very idea of it, and she left the window, going instead to sit on the floor at Marius's knee. It broke the painful concentration that he was faking and he lowered his book to look at her. She put her hands on his knee and rested her chin on them, still avoiding Nicolas's stare. At the gesture, Marius looked up at Nicolas to see that the younger Vampyre was fuming. For all that he could not help it, Marius was not afraid of Nicolas and he put his hand on Elena's head, stroking her silky curls with a loving hand, savoring the sentiment. She closed her eyes and sighed, this being one of the many times that she wished for it all to end so she could be at peace. Nicolas felt it in her and rose angrily, taking it as her constant ungratefulness at her having been turned, before he stormed from the room to also enter the dismal night. Marius felt it as well, but for the sorrow that it truly was and it also saddened him.

"Could we all have changed our fates," he began, "Surely we would have."

"And if you had done it sooner, I would not have to be here now," she agreed.

"No, you would not. All would be quite differently."

A silent moment passed before Elena spoke again.

"Were you ever in love, Marius?"

"A few times." He admitted it without hesitation.

"Did you turn any of them?"

Bitter regret filled him at the question and the memory it invoked reduced his voice to a whisper.

"Only once. Never again."

Elena lifted her head and turned to look at him, his hand remaining on her.

"What is it I feel?" she dared to ask him, thinking of William just enough for Marius to know of what she meant.

"It is not *that*," Marius insisted, his voice low, though he feared that it might be.

"Is it not?" She looked as if to cry and the emotion was intense, almost uncontainable. Marius dropped his book onto his lap and sat forward, taking her head in both hands. For once it was not anger on the matter that showed in his expression, but desperation.

"*Do not think of it here! Do not ever have those thoughts here!* Elena, *please!*"

"I cannot help them!" She grasped his hands and pulled them from her cheeks. "I cannot make them stop! What can it be, if not *that?*"

He pulled her suddenly up into his arms and held Elena with a crushing tightness.

"It will pass, my sweet," he whispered, hoping hard that he was correct. "It will pass with time. Maybe much time, but let it leave you."

Elena could not fathom how it could, the emotion rooted so deeply within her, it was impossible to imagine it some day not being there.

"Do you not understand any of this?" he asked her.

"How can it harm?" She pulled away to look at him. "To love? How can it possibly?"

"Because it is not love," he insisted. "It is not possible."

She shoved away from his embrace so hard it landed her on her feet, well out of his reach.

"You do not *want* it to be possible," she stated, her depression now replaced by the clarity of his jealousy. Marius stood.

"For so many reasons it cannot be."

"For so many reasons, it *should*!" she differed, before turning to leave the room. He followed after her and she stopped at the door, his hand never making contact with her.

"Do not leave the house tonight." She saw his hand rise with worry, but still he would not touch her.

"And the consequences if I do?"

"*Please*, just stay! We shall see Rigel tomorrow night. We can consult him then. You will get your answers, I promise this to you, Elena!"

"I have already consulted him, Marius. And he knows little more than you."

She left him without another word and unconvinced by his pleading. There was still such a great part of her that welcomed harm, for such was her life just then, it would be a great alternative to the confusion and anguish of her current state.

Elena did not bother with a cloak, the rain pouring down now and soaking her with its fall. It would have once felt refreshing to her, but the unseasonable warmth instead met her skin with a numbness. She hurried off into the trees, ignoring that Tavin and Nicolas could be close by and wishing instead for William's arrival. She found him with ease, as he had been watching for her as well, and his lips met her rain-splashed cheeks with anxious kisses.

"How fair you?" he asked her, sensing her darkened mood. But he also felt the questions in her and loathed that he knew their meeting would be short as usual.

"The party is tomorrow night," she said instead, her head lowered as she toyed with his shirt.

"So it is."

She could feel his heart beginning to race through the thin and wet fabric and it made her nearly forget all else she had to say.

"Do not show there, William," she requested.

"You do not want me to?"

"Yes, of course I want you to. But they are becoming more aware of you. Marius especially, because I cannot keep my thoughts to myself."

"And what thoughts are those?" William was half-intrigued, half-pleased and without question fearful of what she would answer with.

"They are not for mentioning, William. Just, take care, and do not come."

She looked up at him when he did not say anything, and she groaned at the tenderness in him, wanting to devour it out of him as her desire did to her inside.

"Most assuredly, I will be there," he promised, seeing how inflamed she was by him, and how it tempted him as well. He grinned at her then, loving that he so easily stole her composure. She could not help smiling back, the glow from him contagious.

"Please, William. For your own sake."

"For my own sake. I would not dream of letting a night pass without seeing you, when I do not have to. I will be most careful, does that make a difference."

All reasoning and wanting of protecting him were waning and Elena's smile dropped when William's did, the serious tone of his expression again full of his desire for her and hers reflecting it.

"Will you not speak your thoughts to me?" she asked him, her voice hushed.

"Can you not hear them?" he whispered.

"Are they the same ones of which your eyes speak?"

"They are."

William lowered his head just a bit, his kiss stopped before it could reach her awaiting lips, the shattering sound of Tavin's voice driving the interruption between them like an axe.

"It is best that you get back, Elena."

She tore away from William to turn to the Vampyre, her regret of being caught only as severe as it was for Nicolas having seen her as well. She glanced behind her at where

William had stood, but he had vanished. She turned back to the others, not knowing what to say and she was greeted with a wrath in Nicolas's eyes beyond any she had ever before seen. And though he had not liked what they had happened upon, Tavin kept neutral—fearful only for her safety—and he reached out to take Elena's hand, pulling her along with him when she accepted his. Nicolas did not move to follow them until Tavin looked back at him.

"Let us go," he said firmly. And after another moment of remaining like stone, for so irate was he that Nicolas could not bear to move, he did at last, coming along with them but a few paces behind.

The walk back to the fortress was heavy and choking with silence, Elena feeling her blood run icy and scorching and chilled again with her thoughts. They were not fully into the foyer before Nicolas grabbed hold of Elena's arm and tore her from Tavin's unsuspecting grasp. He turned immediately at the loss of her hand in his and at her gasp, Elena fighting hard to gain release from Nicolas. But his hands were like vises, moving to take her one by the throat and the other entangling roughly into her hair at the back of her head.

"Let her go—!" Tavin demanded, his anger showing for the first time in front of Elena.

"*Never!*"

Nicolas dragged Elena to her vault and shoved her against her coffin, forcing her head down so she could see that he had destroyed the lock on it.

"Feeling safe *now*?" he raged at her. "And for what? For whom you have been pursuing—you do not deserve to feel safe!"

"What is this?" Marius shouted, having followed at the alerting sounds outside of the library. The surprise arrival of him took Nicolas off guard and Marius shoved him away from Elena with effective separation. Tavin joined them in catching up as well.

"You will never handle her in such a way again, Nicolas!" Marius swore. "Else it shall be the ending of you!"

"Would you say so, did you know what I do of her?" Nicolas fought back.

"If it is of William you speak, then stay your tongue! Nothing will come of it!"

"*Nothing*?" Nicolas repeated with bewilderment, his dark eyes flashing like mercury. "We caught them in an embrace, Marius—much more than *nothing* about to come of it, had we not stopped them!"

Marius did believe it to be true, but he would not—*could not*—let Nicolas continue insisting that it could have become more.

"She is still a new Vampyre," he contended. "She is bound to make mistakes—" And his eyes set on her where she had fallen and still remained on the stone floor.

"Mistakes! Marius, you have become dangerously daft and as well, you are blind! Do you not realize the danger she puts us *all* in by continuing her association with him? Have you no realization of what destruction she will bring to us, does he not leave her alone? And though it is of seemingly little consequence—her own!"

Marius did also know this to be a gloomy possibility, but he could not help softening to her. He held his hand out to Elena and she took it apprehensively, letting him pull her to her feet. He turned her over to Tavin, the touch of them both on her still gentle and giving her a sense of safety.

"That is something that she and I shall discuss directly," Marius said. "But never again shall I see her at your mercy!"

Nicolas fumed at the words and more so when Marius lifted Elena's chin.

"Did you perchance get your fill while you were out?" he asked. She shook her head slowly, still fearful and wondering how she would safely sleep now that this coffin too was rendered unprotected. Marius looked to Tavin, and without a word, Tavin nodded and pulled his sleeve to give her access to his wrist. Elena accepted it meekly and it further enraged Nicolas.

"What's this madness? She consorts with the filth of the forest—we should only dream in our worst of nightmares to what lengths they have gone—and you enable her, Marius? You should let her starve! And have we not had what we needed from her? We need her no longer!"

He made to start for Tavin, to pull her away, but Tavin turned in time, protecting her and daring Nicolas with the promise of a great fight, to try further. Tavin admitted to himself that he wanted the act of her feeding from his veins at that moment, as much as she needed it for survival. Certainly he would let nothing stop that, could he possibly help it.

110

"You are all traitors!" Nicolas hissed, the venom dripping in his voice. He pushed past Marius to leave the vault, the elder Vampyre taking hold of him with a fistful of his jacket to stop him.

"Do be certain that you are yourself not turned traitor, Nicolas!" he warned. "Harming one of our own is forbidden and do not think that you shall survive if she does not!"

"You have already met your doom, Marius, by this insipid protecting of her folly. And do I have the pleasure of seeing Elena meet hers, I shall have no fear of mine."

He stormed out then, leaving the remaining Vampyres in a frenzy of questionable standing. Elena ceased drinking from Tavin, though she was far from fed. She began to speak, Marius stopping her with the raising of his hand.

"We have spoken enough on this for now," he said simply. He checked the lock on her casket and sighed. "I will have it restored. But for this night, Elena, you will use it at your own risk." When he looked up from it, his eyes went to Tavin, Marius's full of warning. "Do not offer your coffin to her, or you shall be under watch as well."

Without another word, Marius left them. Elena filled with dread and Tavin did not release her.

"Is it true then, Elena?" he asked softly. "Of William—"

"Only that I cannot stay away, and I do not know why," she admitted to him.

"Though you have been so advised against it?"

"Yes. Will it pass? As Marius says it will?"

"Do you want it to?"

And Elena felt in her heart that she did not. When she said nothing in answer, Tavin nodded. He placed a kiss on top of her head and let her go.

"To sleep, Elena. There are others that will know better what next to do with you."

He departed then, his cryptic and promising words settling uncomfortably in her. Elena remained for a few moments more, standing in the corner where Tavin had left her, before she went to her casket. Her hands rested on its edge but she could not get into it—it was an open trap to her. She felt lost, groundless—defenseless. The power she was told that she possessed, she felt had abandoned her. And by the way Nicolas spoke, she was now as vulnerable as anyone else under that roof.

Elena left her vault then and returned upstairs, the drapes as always safely closed. She made her way to them, knowing that daylight was rising behind them. She sank down carefully against the wall between the panes, knowing also that if she so needed, she could pull the fabric aside in defense. So it might take her along with the death of anyone else did they dare to approach her—at least she would not go at the hand of another. It was only with this dismal thought that she was able to sleep there, the aching for William still above all else in her heart.

The uncertainty of her well-being overpowered any sense of caution that William could have had and he dared to cross the gates of the property. Never before had he attempted to, for he felt it would have been pointless, knowing that Elena was likely kept underground. But things were different now, and he had to know for certain that she was unharmed.

The thoughts that ran through his head as he approached were merciless: of what he would do to the other Vampyres, did they hurt her; of what he would do from the grief of it to himself—he could not bear the thought of her no longer being there! He knew he should have let her be. He knew he should have kept watch on her from a greater distance. He knew that he should not have let himself be found out by her. And for all of that it was much too late. He would go to the ends of the world for her now. He would stare death in the face for her—he had done it once already and for her it would be worth a second round.

But William's thoughts were interrupted before he even reached the outermost wall, by the slow and faint sound of her beating heart. He rushed to the built-up stone, and sat down against it, staking his life on it that Elena was just on its other side. How he wished that he could get through the stone, to bring her out of it and assure her safety by being with her at all times. He knew that it would have to wait. For now, this would have to be enough.

# Chapter Twenty-One

The night of the masquerade was soon upon them. The Vampyres dressed in costumed finery, each of them, while as ever, Nicolas stepped out for his own hunt and disregarded the invitation Rigel so graciously extended to him.

Elena dressed in peacock blue brocade, her skirt training behind her like a waterfall, her mask plumed with feathers of the bird whose color she wore. She joined Marius and Tavin in the carriage, the black velvet of Tavin's clothing embroidered with indigo silk in Celtic design and Marius's dark green and violet a lively complimenting to Elena's attire.

They soon reached the ball, Rigel at the carriage to personally greet them, his hands taking Elena's to help her down to the ground and to kiss her gloved hands. They entered the house with their host, the crowd of guests already swarming throughout, Marius and Tavin going off on their own, as they knew Elena to be in good company.

"There are many here that wish to make your acquaintance, my dear," Rigel said to her. "Have you yet fed tonight?"

"I have not," she admitted, thought her heart fell for she did not want for one of his guests in their beautiful gala attire to become her victim. Though, she thought, she would make the unfortunate exception, just for the sake of being in the comfort of his safer presence. Before she could say much more, he led her upstairs and into the bedchamber where the young child had been a few weeks before. In her place lay a gentleman, his eyes closed as he babbled in delirium. Elena was at once drawn to him, her mask removed. But she was hesitant and she looked up at Rigel as he stood with his hands clasped and waiting patiently for her to proceed.

"He is not well?" she asked, her fingers feathering over the man's snow-white hair and the life-worn furrows at his brow.

"Sadly, he suffers from a brain fever. He has no one left to mourn for him. You may take what you need in good conscience."

Elena sighed, the man awakening enough to take her hand as he felt her presence there, but his eyes stayed forever closed. The gentle and needful touch startled her for a moment and the word *please* came out on a weak breath. Elena made it a very quick passing for the man.

She stood then at Rigel's hand and sighed again, granting him a smile.

"I can always find whatever it is to suit your taste," he told her, his hands cupping her face. "Always there have been those who are alive but no longer living—not like us, but more like—" And he gestured to the old man, his hand coming back to rest against Elena's neck. "And there will continue always to be those unfortunate souls."

She turned her head, her hand holding his at her cheek and she kissed it. His breath caught at the sentiment.

"You are good to me, Rigel," she said, her eyes returned to him and it was on her next breath to tell him of her concerns with William. And the other Vampyres.

"You have done me a great favor that I cannot equally repay," Rigel began, and Elena suddenly could not speak her mind. "But, I have another favor to ask of you while you are here."

"Of course. What is it?"

"You may decline, if you wish," he started, leaving the room and taking her with him. "I have two guests who are in need of you." This brought a smile to her lips, a mist clouding over her fears.

"To quicken them."

"Yes." And he smiled as well. "Does this interest you?"

"Do you think it wise?"

"They are old friends," he confirmed. "Safe to have around for a few more centuries." Elena's smile grew at his jest and she gave a slight laugh. She thought on it for only a moment and then nodded.

"Yes. I will do it."

"Come then."

He took her into the atrium where two Vampyres—a man and a woman—awaited them. They rose at Elena and Rigel's entrance, both of them humbly awaiting their approach and giving a bowing nod to Elena.

"Elena, this is Sasha, and this is David." They both nodded to her once more. "She has agreed," he told them. David returned to sit, Sasha remaining. She smiled at Elena with bright red painted lips, her china doll face framed by a mass of gold and brown ringlets. She drew her fingers down the side of Elena's cheek gently before the younger Vampyre removed a long black glove to offer her wrist to Sasha. There was the slightest pause with Sasha's momentary disbelief that her own saving act was about to happen, before she accepted Elena's offering. The drawing was quick and Elena's returning of it, as well. Sasha was an ancient as Rigel was, but not so old, her blood more like the taste of cloves and her bite was gentle. The effect on Elena was also not so harsh as it had been with Rigel's quickening, but still left her feeling dizzied.

Sasha took a seat then to recover, her smile perpetual in her blissfulness. David approached Elena then, her other wrist opened to him. She was already beginning to feel light and carefree, and Elena did not see David looking to Rigel, hesitant and fearful. She scarcely saw Rigel as he nodded, and David took her arm gently, his touch echoing his apprehension at what she might be up against. She gasped at the harder bite he gave, though it was beyond the boundaries of pain and it became a numbing grip up her entire arm. She felt slightly weakened from his firm drawing, Rigel's frame at her back ready enough support to keep her standing, and once given a few moments, she quickened David. His blood was as hard as his bite had been, the forceful taste of it making her feel as though she had been given a hard jolt. But the feeling passed and it softened, the full intoxicated sense mixing with the blood of Sasha and coming to her then. David nodded again to her in silence, his eyes now a brightened and smiling cobalt through his black, Empiric-shaggy bangs. Rigel bid their leave, both of them hesitant to go as Rigel still held Elena from behind in his arms, and the two Vampyres at last granted their privacy. The moment the door closed, Rigel's voice came softly against her ear.

"Are you well, my dear?"

"Yes," she whispered, her head spinning as she leaned against him, clutching his arms in her hands and holding them tightly to her.

"Shall you have rest then?" His smile was evident in his tone, for he was rather enjoying the feel of her against him, fresh with the effect the task had just had on her being an added pleasure.

"Yes," At her response, he took her to the settee to let her sit, taking his place at her side, for she did not let go of him immediately. She leaned back after a bit as he did at opposite ends, and they looked at one another in silence for a moment, Rigel's smile never leaving.

"It is a rare thing seeing another Vampyre going through that. You feel no pain from it?"

"None."

"And from them? What have you gained?" Elena thought on his question for a moment, closing her eyes, taking a breath and opening them again before she answered.

"I feel I could tell you the names and origins of nearly all of your present guests."

"Ah. That was Sasha. She is the record keeper of our kind. Even before she was turned, she was known for her perfect memory. It is what saved her from the Spanish Inquisition—she was greatly feared for it, but treasured as well. What else have you acquired?"

"That you are enamored with me, Rigel." His eyes narrowed at her, but his soft grin remained. "You think me more than what Marius was expecting, and it intrigues you," she stated matter of factly. "And there was something special about David—something that scared you, but you no longer have that fear."

"You are in my head, Elena." And she smiled.

"So now no one's thoughts are secret to me," she concluded.

"Some shall still be harder to read, of course, for we make it a necessity to veil what we do not want others to see. But—" He paused to look down at his hands, a still very human habit for him. "There will be those who are willing to let you in."

"Like you?" And his eyes went back to hers, clear and open pathways to his thoughts, and he spoke though he needed not to.

"Like me."

"Shall we sit here then, not speaking?" Her teasing brought his smile to widen.

"Perhaps another time. When we will not be so easily missed." And he could clearly understand in that moment why Nicolas had continued to feed off of her, even after he had turned her and she had finished his quickening. Perhaps it was not solely wanting whatever power she obtained through the quickenings that Nicolas had been after—perhaps it was her charm, her sweetness, her beauty. He dared think it could even be for the simple existence of her. It was hard not to be drawn to her for all of these other reasons, as Rigel could feel himself being pulled in right then as well.

"It would be wise, did we return now," he said, his will stronger than even he thought it could be to say so. They stood and he placed her mask back on her face. He took her wrists, one at a time and sensuously cleaned the blood from them with caressing kisses. The act threatened Elena's composure. He noticed this and refrained, holding her gloves out for her then so she could slip her hands and arms back into them. Rigel's fingers remained on her upper arms where the gloves ended for a lingering moment. He sighed, his smile still soft, and he did not feel like sharing her with the rest of his guests though he knew that he must.

"After you," he said, and she led the way into the hall.

Elena entered the ballroom on Rigel's arm, the dancing and music pausing for the guests to give applause to her and their host in acknowledgement. Rigel gave a wave of his hand for all to continue, Elena smiling at his side.

"That was for you, Elena. So many here are so very pleased that you have come to us," he said, taking her near the center of the room, the others giving them space to dance. "At last, my dance with you," he said in a pleased tone. "And to the music we all can hear!"

Their dancing commenced, much the same way it had only nights before, but even more dreamily to the harp and strings that filled the room with their song. It was a dance that was forever long and still ended as quickly as it had started. Elena could only attribute it to the effects of Sasha and David's blood as it was running through her, the incoherent passage of time having been the former result of such a culprit.

She had scarcely paused to let the swirling room catch up with her when she was released from Rigel and he took his leave of her, before she was taken into another pair of arms. Like Rigel's had been, these were also familiar to her, though they had yet to hold her in dance until now.

"Ah, you are in *that* way again," was said to her in a teasing tone, and they began to move with the music. "It was not terribly difficult to gain entrance to this masquerade, dearest."

Elena smiled and felt the excitement fill her as she recognized the blue eyes behind the black and gray mask. She knew the strong arms that held her and pulled her close as she felt her feet were so far from the ground, though they remained solidly on it.

"William," she said lightly. "You shall not survive the night."

"No?" he played along.

"Certainly *someone* shall whisk you away into the shadows and put their fatal kiss on you by mistake."

"You?" he pressed with hope in his voice, holding her more closely to him and her mask's feathers tickled his neck.

"Not *me*. I already know all about you."

"You think you do."

"I know what you are, what you will become tomorrow night," she whispered against his ear. And then to this she smiled more, despite his words against it, wanting more than ever to be present during his changing.

"Does that amuse you?" he inquired, as it amused him. "Knowing that about me, when nearly no one else does?"

"Rigel knows. Marius knows as well."

"As you can see, little one, I am utterly terrified." She did look into his eyes then, he raising her mask up onto her head. She saw many things in his eyes, but terror was not one of them. She dropped her gaze, his hand slipping down to caress the small curve of her back, bringing her ever closer to him. Her face accidentally touched his bare throat and she gasped softly, but she did not draw away. His head lowered just enough for his lips to be close to her ear.

"I can hear your heart beating even above the din, Elena," he whispered. "It races all the faster—even more than before—the closer you become to me."

She licked her lips, the sudden increased sharpness of her teeth surprising her, but she was close to him—so very close, and those moistened lips brushed against his skin, bringing a very soft growl to rumble from deep within him. The feel of his pulse under her touch, against every sensitive point of her contact with him made her far dizzier than she had been already. He was making it so very easy, tempting her like that.

"Will you not do it?" he asked softly, dipping his head to brush his cheek against hers, leaving the precious burning behind from it. "One little bite—can you not dare yourself?"

"*Not here—*" she whispered, wondering if she shook as hard in his arms with the wanting as she felt she did inside.

"But you would?" And it was just the slightest bit of surprise that edged his words.

"Yes. You tempt me, William—*yes.*"

The song ended then, their steps stopping as well and they had scarcely a moment to separate before Marius was there, grabbing Elena by the arm and leading her away to the portrait room. It was not enough that Marius's face was shadowed by anger—or was it terror? But the multiple eyes that were on them from the paintings in there shook her very nerves.

"*Do not bite him,* Elena!" Marius warned in a hushed and desperate voice. "You do not know what could happen to you!"

"Nothing!" she defended. "*Nothing* will happen to me, Marius, if I bite him!"

"You do not know this!"

"Neither do you," she debated.

"Does your existence mean so little to you?"

"Is *this* to be my existence then, Marius? Having to live as an immortal, but not able to take the risks afforded one?"

"Elena—" he began, more calmly, his disparity in his tone. "Immortal or not: there are still things we *cannot* do. Our restrictions are not merely limited to staying out of the daylight."

"If I can drink the venom that runs through the veins of our kind," she began coldly, and Marius's eyes warned her not to finish.

"Elena—do not—"

"What harm could there possibly be in a Lycan's blood?"

"*Please*, Elena!" he begged of her then. "Promise me that you will not!"

"I have already repaid my debt to you—I owe you nothing, nor to any other Vampyre here. And if my doom is my own doing, then let it be so!"

She began to leave, his hand catching her arm in a tight and painful grasp, and he pulled her close to speak near her ear.

"If you are going to be so foolish, at least do not do it here! You may be powerful, but you are a young Vampyre—you can still die like the rest of us!"

The feel of ice spread through her at those words and she stiffened in his hold. She would not heed his words, but would give respect to Rigel and not impose her *foolishness* in his home. As for the last of Marius's warning, having it now come from him loudly awakened the fear that she had been fighting having at all. He felt this in her and released her arm, realizing that her trust of him was suddenly erased, though it was not himself he had meant to warn her of, and it left a frosty wake as she hurried away from him.

Elena returned to the ballroom, seeking out William but he found her first, taking her back into the safety of his dancing embrace.

"Where is your bite you promised me, my love?" he teased.

Her feet nearly stopped but he continued to carry her through the song. She danced for a moment longer with him, he sensing her deep-set and awakened fear.

"What did he say to you?"

"It was nothing," But her words did not assure him.

"It was *not* nothing," he disagreed with concern. "I can feel you shaking inside."

She spied Nicolas coming for her then, a new and very real, very felt panic filling her. Her dancing stopped immediately.

"You must go, William!" she said desperately, pulling him through the crowd to the opened veranda doors. "Please! *Please!*" He did not argue with her.

"I will go. You be careful. Promise it to me—"

"Yes. *Yes—go—!*"

Nicolas was there just as William disappeared into the night, and took Elena into his arms to dance with her, his lips grazing her neck as they moved, just as hers had done against William's not long before.

"I did not think you were coming here, Nicolas," she said to him. His head lifted and he searched her eyes.

"Does it disappoint you that I have?"

"No," she admitted forcefully, though her surprise still remained in her tone.

He danced her out of the ballroom, out to the empty study and closed the door behind them. He backed her up against the desk in the corner with his hands caging her waist, and licked her lips, tasting blood. It made him smile against her mouth and the feel of such closeness and unable to get William off of her mind made her moan softly.

"You have fed this night?" he asked her.

"Yes," she breathed.

"And quickened?"

"Yes." She could not lie to him, her mind still feeling hazy and the very sound of his voice bringing her senses to slow.

"And was it fulfilling to you?" he said, pressing against her and lifting her up onto the desktop. She gasped at the abruptness of it, her arms holding onto Nicolas for support. He kissed her neck, dragging his fangs across the skin and leaving crimson lines that ran down to her breasts. He caught a trickle of them on his tongue, tasting the ancient blood and smiling when it did not affect him as Rigel's had. He grasped her again around her corseted waist, his hands sliding up beneath her breasts as he bit into the swell of one of them. Elena moaned again, not stopping him, though she knew somewhere in her mind that she ought to.

"Do you want me to have you, Elena?" he asked her at a pause, not yet having taken his fill of her.

"*No*—" she whispered, hypnotically craving his bite more than anything else, and she did not release him but instead held him tightly to her. Nicolas returned his face up near hers, holding her head in his hands, his fists painfully full of her curls, and taking her kiss. Elena tasted the blood he had just taken from her and kissed him to take it back. He bit her there next, sucking on her lip, her faint protest not enough to bring him to stop.

"Nicolas—" she breathed after he let go.

"I miss you in my bed, Elena," he growled. "I miss the way the freshly stolen lives of others taste when I drink them from you—"

She felt the world swirling around her, but barely felt him raising her skirts and parting her pantalets, before sinking down before her. There was the slightest, quick and firm tasting of her that nearly set her off, but his mouth moved to the apex of her hip and thigh, ignoring the carnal craving her body gave for him. The puncture came then and she cried out from it, her fingers digging into his shoulders to keep him there, only the cloth between them keeping her from breaking

121

his skin. He took all that he could from her then, his smirking face staring into hers when he finished. He let her skirt drop with rough disregard, her arms too weak to hold onto him and she toppled off of the desk to his feet like a broken doll.

"You will never belong to anyone else," he growled. "If it is the last thing you ever hear, be certain you hear that!"

He quit the room, leaving her behind and retrieved his cloak. Marius saw him go and suddenly realized that Elena was no longer in the safety of the ballroom. He did not try stopping Nicolas but instead began a frantic search of the other rooms, finding Elena at last where she had fallen, drained nearly dry.

The words *dear God* escaped his mouth, though he struggled to know—what really had God to do with it? Marius knelt with her, clearing her tresses from her face, turning her head and searching for a pulse. She was worse off than she had been the night after her turning, the tears and holes Nicolas had made in her flesh not healing or even beginning to. He gathered her up in his arms just as Rigel entered the room, he rushing to their sides before Marius could say anything to him. They exchanged only a glance before Rigel held the side of her face in one hand, lifting one lid of her closed eyes to see that even the irises were drained of color. It filled him with a panic that he hoped Marius could not sense through his own, for Elena was nearly dead. Only one other time had he seen one of their kind in such a condition—and she had not survived.

"Let me take her," Rigel coaxed softly. "I will fix this."

Marius held her for a moment more, the sorrow he felt countering the fear and he did not want to let her go.

"*Please*—" Rigel whispered. "There is no time!" And Marius reluctantly let him take Elena into his own arms. He turned without another word, only giving a nod for Marius to follow, and Rigel carried her up to his chambers, shutting himself in, with Marius standing guard outside. Rigel made haste to set Elena into the fluffy midst of his bed. He checked to be certain that the doors were locked from the inside, and at once made for his balcony. He closed those doors tightly behind him as well, once he was out into the night air.

He knew what reviving her was going to take and he knew that Elena in her current state, would take it no other way.

It was a quick search, Rigel's return with Elena's cure held in his arms coming in less than an hour. The tiny mewling cries he gently put an end to, not wanting to attract any of the other Vampyres to it, as surely the nearly forbidden treat would have, did they hear it. He sat on the bed with Elena, the newborn placed next to her, silent and in a sleep it would never awaken from. One tiny vein opened, from one tiny arm, and the slow trickle went over Elena's lips and down her throat. It took a very long time to be over and longer still afterwards for Elena's skin to begin warming from the infant's blood.

When it was over, Rigel left her, keeping the doors locked so no one could get in or out, and posting one of his own trust-worthy servants just outside of the room to relieve Marius, and to see to his other guests.

"Will she be alright?" Marius was asking as they went down the winding stairs. His fears had not wavered in even the slightest bit. Rigel shook his head slowly, putting his hand on Marius's shoulder as they walked.

"Only tomorrow night shall tell us."

"*I will kill him*!" Marius could scarcely breathe, as he was so very enraged. At these words, Rigel stopped him.

"Do not. Do not even let Nicolas believe that she has survived what he has done! He has gone too far, I agree, but we do not need him here trying to do it again! Whatever it was that he was intending."

"He was trying to kill her, Rigel. What else could he have possibly been trying to accomplish? I no longer believe that he is enamored with her—he wants nothing but to rid us all of her!"

"It does not appear differently, my friend."

"What then, is to be done with him? He cannot get away with this!"

"*All is fair*—is that not what they say?"

These words did not sit well with Marius and his eyes darkened, a challenge of his own passing into Rigel's eyes. The elder saw this and sighed, closing them for a moment.

"Leave Elena to me. And I will look into dealing with Nicolas as well. But not tonight."

"The others deserve to know about this. We should call them together."

"Not yet. Let us wait until tomorrow. If she does not—" And even he could not say the word. "We will call upon the others if we need to. They will want to know why he did this. I do not believe that any of them are even aware of William, but for your boys. Now is not the time for explaining to the rest of them, her acquaintance with him."

Marius clenched his teeth together but finally nodded in agreement.

"Very well. And William? What are we to do about him?"

"Nothing. He is not ours to do anything about. But do be certain that he also never finds out about this—keep Nicolas from telling him, as I am certain he shall try for the sake of his own selfish means, and to entice him into battle. William is the only one of his kind that I have ever known of here, and though we cannot be certain there are not more, he seems the only one brave enough to interact with one of our own."

"Brave—or foolish? I have no explanation for his interest in her, and that makes him a threat to her safety. And perhaps to us!" Rigel did not bring it to light that perhaps William's only interest in Elena was simply that he was drawn to her for who she was. He was certain that Marius was aware of it already—how could anyone, and William as no exception help themselves of it?

"Regardless—we do not need that kind of war in any of our houses." He paused for a moment in thought. "William has been after her for a very long time, I know. It is fortunate for her that you turned her first. I fear that had he gotten to her, whether he meant to or not—he would have shred her into ribbons." And then half jestingly, "Could you not have better kept them apart, Marius?"

"I tried. She will do as she pleases and there have been enough close calls already. I cannot believe that Nicolas's greed for her blood would be enough for such an act. He knew of William's closeness with her, though I do not believe it was beyond what any of us witnessed, for him to warrant having done this to her."

"They have not—?" Rigel's fears of Elena's interactions with William set him off into his own panic. "She has not—?"

"She keeps mentioning it. But I think not yet." And there was a silent pause as Rigel though over the situation, and he remembered then that Sasha and David had been quickened with ease and no repercussions.

"If she were to bite him—"

"She will *not*," Marius swore, though with all of the fire behind his words, he could not promise them. "So help me, she will not!"

"But *were* she to—" Rigel hesitated, nodding to a few of his guests as they passed by. "And Nicolas were to feed from her then—"

"Are you mad?"

"*If* she were to survive it, and then—"

"There will never be the chance—I will not let her have it!" And this Marius did vow.

"She may do this whether you want to keep her from doing so or not, my friend. Try as we might, aside from making a prisoner of Elena—and I know you do not wish that for her—there is nothing we can do to stop it."

"Is there not?" Marius begged to differ.

"Perhaps we should let it happen."

"You *are* mad!" Marius felt his heart catch at his friend's words. "You try to save her this night, only to hope for her to take *his* blood?"

"It would be like poison."

"*Exactly.*"

"But perhaps not to *her*." Marius took a moment for Rigel's words to sink in, the very thought of what he had been implying ludicrous. Rigel and Elena thought very much alike sometimes, Marius noticed. Rigel sighed again.

"Why are you so insistent that she do this, Rigel? That she even *can* do this?"

"Marius—" Rigel paused, knowing that what he had to say would not likely set well with his friend. But what more could he not say to him? "I had her quicken David tonight."

Marius felt his heart stop at the admission, but he tried not to think of the other times—the other failed attempts that had been made for their other friend. And he had seen Elena since it had to have happened, and she was no different to him for it, save her belligerence.

"After all of the other times—you tried *her*? Without telling me of it first?"

"Would you have let me otherwise, Marius?"

"Never!"

"I knew this and I admit the risk involved. But David needed her, probably more than the rest of us, and we need him. She managed it well enough and it did no more than weaken her for a few moments. No other that we have allowed to try, has been able to do it for him, and she passed the test."

Marius let out an exasperated breath, his hand going to his face. There were too many thoughts fighting for his attention, too many fears and too many wishes. This one of David and the former failures, and Elena having done well could not be one to dwell on just then.

"And he is alright from it?"

"Quite. I am certain that he is more relieved than anything, to know that he has just been given another chance."

"Still, I cannot believe you put her to it. And so soon."

"If not tonight, then when? Would there be any good time to test it?"

"I suppose you are right, Rigel." Marius sighed and Rigel held his friend's face in his hands.

"Let us all just get through this night and see tomorrow with new eyes."

"Dawn is not far away," Marius began. "And yet I do not think I shall sleep at all. I shall be waiting on needles to hear from you, Rigel. At the first moment possible, as soon as night falls, send word."

"Of course, Marius."

He saw Marius off shortly there after, and as he was quite exhausted from the night, Rigel was not at all disappointed when it came to its end and everyone left. In fact, he could not wait for the moment and once the last carriage had left his gates, he promptly returned to Elena's side.

She was unconscious, and once he had closed the heavy drapes at the windows and around the berth, he climbed onto it with her. It would ordinarily have been a temptation to have her there, but as she was, he could only hold her in his arms and hope that what he had done—what she would hate knowing he had done to her, would work. There was a chance that it might not, but the very young, very fresh life he had sacrificed for her would help, as there was nothing else that he could think of that would.

## Chapter Twenty-Two

It was well after the moon had risen, before Elena even began to stir a little. Rigel remained still, not sure she had actually awaken and afraid to know if he had imagined it. He continued holding her as he had been unmoving for hours, and praying in any way a Vampyre could instead of sleeping himself. She spoke before moving and the faint sound of her voice startled him.

"What has happened to me?"

He sighed and tightened his hold on her for a moment before releasing her and tipping her face up to his to look it over. Her eyes were still glazed, but the color was slowly coming back into them. The deathly gray pallor of her skin was completely gone and her tone was perfect ivory, the blue of her lips was tinted with rose.

"How did you manage it?" she asked. "Bringing me back. I still feel it in my veins—like nothing that I have ever had before." She paused and he waited, knowing that there was more that she would say, and then she did:

"What kind of blood could taste so very sweet and be so terribly potent?" And as her own words came, the answer did as well and she began to shake her head, the real wetness of the baby's tears welling up to make her own.

"Yes," was all that Rigel said, gently stroking her hair, hoping to soothe the storm that would come of it. But knew he could not.

"*No*," she whispered. "You did not—say you did not!"

"It was the only way, my dear. I am sorry."

"*No!*" she insisted, sitting up and covering her face in her hands, the tears turned to blood dripping through them. "God, no!"

"I knew you would be upset, Elena. I am sorry," he said again, truly meaning it. "But it was the only way. You would have been lost to us otherwise."

"Then you should have let me be lost!"

He supposed that she might be right, despite his and all other Vampyres' selfish wishes against her own.

"You have too much conscience for a Vampyre," he stated instead, unable to show his sympathy as he sat up with her.

"Have I?" *And William*—thoughts beyond the simple drinking of his blood crossed her mind, loudly enough for Rigel to pick up on them.

"*Do not do that*—what you are considering! It is unthinkable!"

"Is it?" she challenged him.

She rose from the bed and went to the balcony doors in a breath, Rigel right behind her. He turned her to face him.

"You can put no stop to this," she said, as his thumbs brushed under her eyes to clear the tears as they still fell, unbeknownst to her. He agreed with her but said nothing, only fear showing in his eyes for her. It was the unknown that terrified him and he could not hide that from her.

"The *unknown*," she scoffed bitterly. "It is all and everything that we are made of, Rigel. Why are we not ashamed that we shy away from it?"

Her words were the shaking of their very foundation—built over and upon centuries—making up what they all were, and it brought Rigel a greater fear to realize that she was right: there was more danger behind Nicolas finding Elena still alive and taking the newborn's blood from her than there could be in William's interactions with her—no matter what it was that transpired between them. Rigel could only imagine it and wished the thoughts from his mind, as he could not be a part of them.

"Do not go, Elena. You will not be safe."

"I have no care for *safe*."

Rigel wanted to argue with her, he wanted to be the one to protect her, but he had done all that he could and he knew that her heart was elsewhere. For this, his was only a slightly milder envy than Marius's—though envy nonetheless, and it kept Rigel at the balcony wall, watching in the direction Elena then fled. And though it would be that night that they would lose her, he knew she would be safer did he not condemn her going to the Lycan. Not he, nor even Marius could protect her from harm as William could. It was all that kept him from going after her.

# Chapter Twenty-Three

The autumn moon—the first of the season greeted Elena when she stepped out under its light. She paused to close her eyes for a moment, pretending that it was the sun instead, for its shine was so very bright. She opened them again and started along her way, knowing that she ought to stay clear of William, to let him deal with his transformation in peace, but curiosity won her over. It led her feet along its uncharted path, far from the fortress and anywhere else she had yet seen.

It was not hard to find him, though she had traveled quite a distance, for the scent of blood was so heavy on the air, it may as well have been a trail plainly spilt along the ground.

She could hear Rigel's voice in her head still—words both spoken and those that had not been. She still heard how he had pleaded for her not to leave his home that night, fearing what could happen to her, but she could not stay. Not even for the easing of the hunt that his hospitality granted her, and not even though the rich blood of the infant would keep her full for a long while. No, Rigel could not stop her, and he had known it. Marius would not reach Rigel's manor in time to try to stop her either, and Elena was certain that even if he had tried, he too would have been unsuccessful.

Rain threatened, the sky full of scattered clouds ready to burst and bring forth a storm of droplets. Elena hoped it would not affect the trail she had found, and though she knew that William did not want her to see him transformed, she craved the chance for just a glimpse. The trail held strong, and she soon came to its end. She found herself outside of a deserted and falling-apart barn, a vagrant busily gathering wood for a meager fire. William stood just breaths away from the man in the darkness, William's back to a wall as he seemed to be bracing himself and holding his breath. But then the change came so quickly, and he was so captured by it, he did not notice that Elena had found him. She remained in the shadows as the clouds cleared from the moon and William began to clutch his head with both hands, the metamorphosis seemingly painful to his human self, though he did not make a sound. Elena scarcely breathed herself, almost wanting to stop what he was going through for his sake, though it was far too fascinating for her to move from hiding and there would be no stopping it no matter what she did.

It was very few seconds later that he became the great beast she had seen for the first time a month before, and before his intended victim could even take notice that he was being stalked, William attacked him, going at once for the man's throat.

There was a great spraying of blood and very little struggle, the death certainly quite fast and too much of a surprise for any kind of defense to be made. Elena watched as William tore the man's flesh with his long teeth, broke into his ribs with long, clawed fingers and ate his heart while the organ was still alive. She thought only for a moment of her first killing, thinking it had been very bloody, but the sight before her made her tremble far more where she stood, made her mouth water and her own hunger nearly blinding. The dead man hung limp in William's grasp, the beast of him still tearing and feeding in turn until he seemed to have had all there was of the corpse.

The transformation back to himself as the moon was covered came quickly and William had dropped the body to the ground in disgust, his own form now half crouched over it, and the beast's fur falling away like smoke to leave only his smooth, bare skin. Elena gasped softly and let the breath back out, William hearing her immediately and pinning her through the cloud-made darkness. They only held one another's gaze for a moment before William remembered himself and hurriedly pulled his victim's cloak around his own nakedness. Elena was already rushing to him as he was standing, his embarrassed apology coming forth.

"Forgive me—" he was muttering, trying to wipe the blood from his face, and unable to meet her eyes. But she had smelled the blood, had seen it, needed it—needed *him*—and Elena came at him so swiftly, he had to catch her in his arms to stop her from colliding into him and knocking him down into the pools of blood at their feet. Her face went to his neck immediately as it had the night before, her tongue flickering against his flesh to taste it, fighting hard not to bite through the stranger's blood to get to William's. He gasped, not wanting her to stop.

"Please—Elena. You cannot do that—" But his hands remained on her arms, holding her there.

"Why not?" she breathed. "I will not hurt you, I promise! Only a taste, William—I want of you so terribly— *please*—"

"You would be forever bound to me, Elena. I cannot risk that. If your kind ever found out about it—"

"How could they know?" she asked, still wanting to be close to him and he still holding her just enough away.

William pushed the cloth of her cloak away and with gentle force and unable to help his own desires, cupped one breast in his hand, running his thumb over her skin and feeling the holes Nicolas had made over her heart. Elena's eyes lifted, showing that she had not expected them to still be there, though it was a fleeting detail for William's touch on her, and his growing passion-caught breaths took her attention.

"Because he feeds on you. He would know by the taste of my blood."

"He won't! I'll not let him have my blood again!"

"Go, Elena. They will not want you here with me. Get back to your fortress before you are caught and it is too late."

An incredible aching far worse than any other began to grow in her for William and the thought of leaving him made her feel ever more weakened.

"I've no wish to leave you right now!" she protested still, trying to get closer to him. "And I should *not* go there— Nicolas thinks me dead, I am certain!"

"And why would he think that?" William inquired, now growing more concerned for her safety, were she to leave him.

"He tried to bleed me dry after you left the masquerade—"

William's eyes sparked with apprehension and anger and his grip on her tightened for a moment before he turned her face one way and then the other. Her skin was alabaster pale but glowing, flawless.

"Lower," she said softly of the bite, her hand dropping down to the bend in her hip. The rage in William at Nicolas grew hard within him, though he kept it from his touch on her, his thoughts distracted by her touching of herself.

"Because he has known that you see me in the night?" William asked. "Because he has discovered us for himself."

"It does not matter now," she insisted, pulling his hand from her face and placing it back on her ribs. "He thinks me gone."

131

"How did you survive it?" And William could see that something more was different in her and she was alive with innocent blood that made even his hunger rekindle. Her hand went to his rough cheek, warm with his victim's blood. Her touch and the look in her eyes for him made the answer unimportant just then and he sighed inwardly at the sweetness of it.

"Are you not scared of the rest of them now?" he asked instead. "Of the consequences of being here with me?"

"I am not scared. What more could they do to me? They cannot keep me from being here with you. Nothing matters but that *you* would want me here."

William knew what the many consequences could be, but dreaded to say. His silence made his known answer of it seem false of what she was asking, and a heavy and uncomfortable fear that he had made up his excuse brought Elena's steps to retreat. Their eyes remained still locked and it struck her then—perhaps he truly did not want her—?

She began to back away with force, but as their fingertips touched, William realized her fear. He grabbed her hand and pulled her back, capturing her mouth with his, a different but very fully awakened thirst in her drinking from his kiss. He brought her away from the mess he had made, keeping her kisses coming, and then held her head, dropping the bloody cloak and unclasping hers so it fell as well. Her hands lowered to touch the bared skin of his chest and arms, feeling the blood on him, still sticky and warm from the heat of him. She tried to draw her lips from his, wanting to taste it again, but he kept her from it. It was the slightest pained sound that she made at the denial of it, but he moved her against the side of the barn, his body gently trapping hers. His touch was soft, direct, even as he lifted her skirts, staying with her, their fevered kisses continuing. He gave pause to bring her arms up to encircle his neck, his soft blue eyes coming to hers, now silver with her inner fire. He waited no longer and lifted her onto him easily, the suspected warmth of her surprisingly great, and the gasp she emitted foretelling that all he had wondered of her was indeed true. Her legs wrapped around his waist tightly and he pressed her to the wall, moving more deeply into her. William drew another kiss from her, Elena pulling away first, nearly too lost in pleasure to think.

"What if you change again?" she breathed.

"I cannot. Not while we are like this."

132

"But say you did—?" He grinned, his eyes smoldering with passion.

"I would eat you up."

"William—please—" she whispered. He gave a thrust that made Elena tip her head back with a pleasured cry, her fangs sharp, eager. The sight of them was nearly too much for William, the thought of their piercing into him making him growl against her, his face buried into her neck, for he wanted it as well. Elena could feel it in him and lifted his face to turn his head, her mouth going to his throat. He groaned, hating to stop her.

"Not yet, my love," he whispered. "Not this time—"

"You do not want it of me?"

"*Yes*, I want it!" His eyes turned back to hers. "But we must wait. Until I know for certain you are safe, and not until the moon has passed."

Elena pushed no more, letting him continue their ardent engagement until William brought their passion to an end with his climax.

He lowered her carefully onto her feet, Elena's legs shaking beneath her as she held onto him, and the blood coursing through her veins making her unbearably dizzy. William sat with her, holding her in his arms as scattered images of his transformations flashed through her mind. She rested her head against his chest and held onto him. William lowered his head down into her hair and smiled, his breathing slowing as he relaxed.

"Are you alright, my love?" he asked her.

"Mm. I think I shall enjoy being dead to them," she said lightly.

"They truly think you are?" he asked.

"Nicolas must, as it seemed his intention and he left me at what I am certain was the worst of it. But Rigel knows I still live and he will tell Marius."

William sighed with concern at the idea of a search being made for her. His arms embraced around her tightly and he kissed her head.

"You must be so very careful now, dearheart," he warned.

"I must only be certain that they do not feed on me anymore. Aside, they cannot hurt me." Elena smiled and William did as well, sadness hanging on his heart.

"They could. Now that we have—" Elena interrupted him with a kiss and he smiled under it.

"We are bound, my William."

"Nearly. Enough to infuriate them further." William looked into Elena's eyes. "They do not take well to our kinds—*acquainting* ourselves with one another."

"So I have heard. But I do not understand."

"Nor I."

"They truly know nothing of what they fear, William."

"All the more reason for them to feel they must have that fear."

William sighed again as did Elena and she rested her head against his chest.

"You grow sleepy, my darling?"

"Yes," she admitted.

"We must get you somewhere safe, Elena. The night is so close to having passed."

She nodded in agreement.

"Nicolas will have gotten in by the time I arrive to the fortress—"

"What's this? You have changed your mind? You are not thinking of going back there—?"

"My coffin is there, and I know it is otherwise protected." And after a moment of pondering, she added, "I do not think Marius will try to harm me, do I show there. He will be quite surprised at it, I am thinking. And then I can leave before any of them awaken tonight."

"I do not want you to go back there," William said, apprehensively. Elena sensed this and cradled his face in her hands. She melted into the blue sea of his eyes and he warmed again from the hunter green fire in hers.

"I do not want it either. But until we think of another way—"

"I know."

Elena smiled playfully.

"It has a lock," she said of her casket. William laughed softly.

"Use it, my love. Do promise me that you will."

"Of course, my William, for you." She stared into the crystal of his eyes for a long moment and sighed. "The day will be forever long until I see you again."

"As it will be for me," he agreed. Her eyes grew smoky at him with rekindled passion.

"I wish so very much that we had more time," she whispered, rubbing her cheek against his. He rubbed back, the motion leaving the pleasant burn against her skin.

"As do I, my Elena."

"But then—have we not our lifetimes now?" she asked, and William held her tightly and close once again.

"Of course, my love."

But their parting had to come, and William let Elena go, keeping so very closely behind her and never letting her out of the sight of his watchful, protective eyes.

# Chapter Twenty-Four

Elena left William with great reluctance and made her way back to the fortress, William still keeping close watch on her but from a greater distance than he cared to be. She was close—so very close, but the sun was threatening to rise, though the night's clouds had lingered. Even they were beginning to dissipate, removing any protection that Elena might have to shield her from the deadly rays.

She reached the castle, turning back to where she suspected William to be hiding from spying eyes and blew him a kiss. He smiled at seeing her do it, aching to have the sentiment straight from her lips to his own, but he would have to wait until nightfall for it. Elena stepped up onto the front landing, and her hand fell onto the latch. The realization of her vulnerable state began to run through her before she even tried to lift it, and when she did, she found that it was tightly secured—there would be no way to get inside.

She felt the panic rise within her, but tried to remain calm, knowing that of course it would be locked—no one was expecting her to be there! But she was proven terribly wrong when the drapes within the windows moved, and the fair skin of Nicolas's face showed through the glass. His expression was one of surprise at first, but at seeing Elena at the door, his black eyes narrowed and his smile fast became a sneer. She felt ill, hopeless and she sensed her end was truly near when he dropped the cloth abruptly and disappeared from sight. But then the lock was unbolted and he opened the heavy wooden door, leaving the ironwork gate of twisted horns and tulips between them still tightly locked.

"Well, Elena," he said, not hiding the disdain or the shock in his voice though he was quite pleased that she was outside just then.

"Nicolas—please, let me in—the sun is coming—!"

"*The sun is coming*—" he mocked. "The sun *is* coming, Elena. You are just in time to see it. As I am certain you have no doubt missed it, I do so hope that you enjoy your revisiting and last sight of it."

And before she could say anything more, Nicolas slammed the door shut and she heard the bolts close in. She could not stand there and bother to pound on it. She knew that Marius and Tavin would be fast asleep in their caskets and most likely they would not hear her. There was the slightest possibility that Marius might, but there just was no time. Elena could not wait for the sound to penetrate his coffin—and there would be no time for getting into hers.

Elena turned and ran across the bridge, across the stretch of property for the trees—bare but for the grass—and all of it seeming greater in length than she remembered it, for she was quickly growing weak in the rising light. There would not be time to get to Rigel's and as she had left him, she was not so certain that he would assist her again. And most definitely not if he knew that she had just been with William.

And where was William?

The sun was lifting rapidly and the clouds were bursting from trying to hide it. Elena drew her hood up, holding it tightly around her and concealing her hands in the cloth. But she was still too far from the shade of the trees, and she knew that even once she had reached them, it would not be long before the sun's rays would come filtering in through the falling leaves. She needed darkness. She needed sleep.

And then it broke through, the heat and intensity of the sun coming down on Elena with a pressure that brought her to her knees. She could not stand again and she had to let go of her cloak to crawl, the light hitting the skin of her hands and turning it red and then white hot like ash, the swirling of smoke and the scent of burning flesh rising from it. Elena felt cold blood dripping from her eyes and her nose, saw it drop down into the grass below her and she began to ache all over as though she were being drawn apart from every joint. She was not even close to shade and she would not make it in time, so quickly was her strength leaving her and her skirts only further hindered the speed of her meager crawl.

It was to be her end and she accepted the fact, telling herself that it was a blessing that would release her from the curse she had involuntarily been bestowed with. It was the least she deserved for ingesting the infant's blood—for ingesting anyone's blood. And she lay down in surrender to let the sun devour her at last—for certainly she now had no choice—and thinking only of the pleasantness of William and wishing him there to hold her as she died.

# Chapter Twenty-Five

Great swiftness was not something that usually lasted for William once the moon had begun to wane, but so fresh and full was it still in the dawn, and as it remained in the distant sky, it granted him the offering. He had not left nor had he lost sight of Elena for a moment. He had seen her approach the locked door and he had seen Nicolas turn her away. And William had seen her trapped under the brutal sun.

William was upon her in mere moments after she had hit the ground, taking care as he scooped her up into his arms that he was not exposing any more of her into the light. He ran with her then, taking them deep into the woods, far from the fortress, far from where they had spent the hours of the night. He did not stop until they were somewhere even he had never ventured before.

It was a small house that he found for them, empty and decrepit, but it was dark and it offered a cellar void of the slightest bit of light. William carried Elena down into it, left her to find a solitary candle, dusty and dirty in its stick. She made no sound as he pushed back her hood and lifted her head. She slept as deeply as though dead and when he checked for a pulse, he saw the state of her burns, the flesh having turned black. William tried not to become discouraged, reasoning that she could regenerate and heal herself if given time.

And blood. She was going to need blood.

He would not be able to get her any until nightfall and she certainly could not go anywhere until then.

William sighed and sat against the wall, drawing Elena into his arms. She stirred just the slightest bit, whimpering almost inaudibly.

"I'm sorry—" she breathed.

"Shh—"

"I am sorry—I am sorry—"

"Shush, love. Rest now and save your strength. You are safe," he whispered to her.

Elena dropped off again into slumber from the fatigue of her body trying to heal itself, and she did not budge again until night. And even then, she scarcely gave proof that she was not dead to the world.

"My sweet—" William said to her, pushing the tresses back from her face.

"William—" she whispered. She tried to move but could not even raise her hand to his cheek, and the burn had not changed. She could not go out and hunt, he knew, and in her condition, Nicolas would likely be on her like the vicious predator that he was.

"Elena, what am I to do for you?" he asked, uncertain as to whether or not she even heard him.

"I cannot leave here like this," she managed. "They will find me. I've not the strength—"

"Then you must stay. I will return soon." He kissed her brow and left her then, heading out into the darkness and wishing the moon would bestow its curse on him that night. He knew he needed to find her a victim, but without the beast to drive him, William knew that he had not the heart to kill anyone.

For this, he knew not what to do. What he needed then for Elena's sake was advice. He knew where he could find it, though he dreaded it. But this was for no other reason than to help his precious lady. And for her survival he would try.

# Chapter Twenty-Six

The waning moon still afforded him some assistance with speed, letting William reach the fortress gates in a short time, and it was not long that he had to wait before Marius came out and William found him.

"Our Elena lives?" he asked apprehensively, keeping his distance from William.

"She is not *ours*!" William argued. "She is now *mine*! You lost her forever when Nicolas cast her out to burn to death in the sun—and *you let him*!"

"I did not know of that!" Marius insisted, "Only that she had not returned to us when I awoke, and Rigel did not know of her whereabouts." But William was leery to believe him. "I had assumed—I had *hoped*—that she had found her way to safety somehow."

Marius could see that William was much too caught up in his feelings for Elena, and as something more was different with him, Marius could tell that William was not much concerned about instigating a physical fight with the Vampyre.

"Where is she now?" Marius asked more gently instead. "No. You will not tell me that, will you?"

"Not in a million of your lifetimes."

"But you have her. What Nicolas did to her at Rigel's—and what you say he tried to do—she has still survived it? She is well?"

"She has and no, she is not."

William saw the change in Marius's eyes, concern now lit up in them as well.

"She is hurt?"

"Nicolas knows she is alive. Or was as of this morning. He'll believe it still, not having found a pile of ash that should have been Elena on your grounds."

Marius sighed heavily and with great troubling.

"I will see to it that he believes that she did not survive this morning. At least I can try to convince him for a while. But Nicolas was set on destroying her the night of the masquerade," Marius stated.

"It does appear to be so," William agreed scathingly.

"Once he discovers that the remains I will have put on the lawn do not belong to her, he will be after her once again."

"And have you any advice, Marius? On how I am to undo this damage he has caused, or how to further keep her safe? Or do you agree with him? Do you too wish her destroyed? I cannot become a monster tonight, though could I, I might bring about all of your endings."

"*No!*" Marius spat. "I do *not* also wish that of her! I have never wanted that for her!"

"Then tell me why you have not taken greater care to keep yourself better hidden from me this night. You want to know does she live. You want to know where I have her. What else is it that you have to say to me, Marius, that is not a question?"

Marius hesitated, not wanting to say anything to William but knowing that he must, for Elena's sake—and for her protection, though he had no proof that it would keep her safe.

"*Speak!*" William raged. "We may lose her this night yet!"

"I do not want this for her!" Marius countered. "For I do not know what it will do to her, but I have been advised—" He paused, lowering his voice and taking a centering breath. "I have been told by my elders that I *must* tell you this—"

"And what is it, Marius, I am listening."

"You must give her your blood—" Marius did not finish, the thought of the Lycan's blood destroying her making him feel devastatingly ill.

"Will it not harm her?" William asked, surprised at the Vampyre's words.

"I do not know," Marius admitted. "I fear that it will, and though even she admitted to me of toying with the idea of it, it is clear that there is now no choice in the matter."

"Can I not bring someone to her? Someone to feed from?"

"No. Only you." Marius lowered his head and his voice showed his pain. "It must be you."

"Why, me?"

Marius looked away from William, jealousy deep and dangerous welling up within him. He ignored the question.

"You have stated that she is in a bad way, and that is the advice I must give you now. I cannot offer you anything else." When William said nothing, Marius added, "I will have her coffin moved, William, but you must protect her or she will indeed be lost to us all." His eyes returned to the Lycan's then. "Your involvement with her is entirely forbidden, William. That is not just my wish but it is held by all."

"Then why do you try to help her?" he bit back, completely skeptical of Marius's motives. "*Are* you even trying to help her?"

The Vampyre's eyes lowered again in shame and was he capable of shedding tears, William was positive that Marius would have just then.

"Because I have come to love her in a way that Nicolas can himself never know—in a way that you yourself cannot deny loving her."

"Can I not take her farther away from here? From all of this, and all of your Vampyre *rules*?"

"I cannot recommend it."

"And why is that? You have gotten what you needed from her."

"For six hundred years I waited for her to come, William. She has given me what I needed, yes, but I too need Elena near. I will offer whatever help I can to keep Nicolas away from her, but you shall have to keep her from the castle. She was made there. She will forever be drawn back to it. There is nothing safe in it for her now and it cannot be her home. And so long as she has interest in you, no other Vampyre will harbor her."

"And what of Nicolas? Does your kind not have laws? Is he not to be punished for what he has attempted— *twice*?"

"He has attempted but he has not succeeded," Marius said, his own anger against Nicolas rising. "We cannot touch him."

"But I can."

Marius took steps closer to William, his hand outstretched to him.

"Do not try to! You are powerful when you are changed, William, it is true. But if you do not best him on the first attempt, then she will be his for the taking. He knows of your trailing of her. If he thinks her gone, he will be watching you, hunting you, and he will learn instead that you have her now. Does that happen, he will not stop trying to get to Elena until he has her, and at any cost. You will be no competition to him."

"And how do you know he is not with her now?" William spoke, hoping that his own rising fears were not so noticeable as he felt they were.

"Nicolas sleeps right now but he will be awake very soon. You must get back to Elena now and do not leave her side, *ever* when it is night. She will never be safe so long as he is alive."

"And who is to do away with him if I cannot, if you *will* not?"

"*She* must do it. No one can try but Elena, for no matter any of our feelings on the concern, *she* is the one he has wronged."

"How is she to do this? You give so few answers, Marius."

"Get her well. Get her strong again. The opportunity will present itself at Nicolas's own hand." Marius turned his head and paused to listen for a moment before he spoke again. "You've not much time to get back to her. Do not let her outside. He cannot cross any threshold you are within without your invitation. But if she is alone or she is out of doors—"

"I am on my way to her," William interrupted. "Make her casket available to me at once."

He did not wait to hear more before he left Marius behind and hurried back to his beloved.

William reached the little house quickly and paused upon entering the door. He waited and listened, and breathed the air: nothing was different. He took the stairs and found Elena, still as he had left her and half asleep.

"William—" she said at the flickering of the candlelight he carried.

"I am here."

She smiled, now at ease though the emptiness in her belly ached and filled her every inch. William looked at her for a long moment, dreading the risk of what he was told to do. He tried to think only on Elena having wanted to bite him, of how it had filled her with a sweet and passionate desire. She had never wanted to do it to kill him, and he knew this. She had no knowing if it would harm him—just as he did not know. He supposed it was what kept them from already trying. But Marius was right and there was no choice now, and the longer William hesitated, he knew the weaker she would become.

He gathered her up into his arms and took his dagger from the sheath on his leg, drawing it swiftly across his arm. Elena reacted to the smell of it at once, her brows coming together in confusion. When William brought his arm closer to her and let the blood drip onto her lips, she gasped, realizing from where it was coming, and her mouth closed tightly in protest.

"Elena, my love, you must," he whispered before she could further refuse. "Just a bit. Do not be afraid—"

"*You* are afraid, William—" she said, trying to wipe the droplets from her mouth before they could go in, and seeing the tracks of his veins glowing brightly when she opened her eyes.

"I am," he admitted. "But try. Only a few drops—"

Their eyes met and she could not look away from them. Certainly she was not ready to leave him, did the result turn out terribly wrong.

"Does it bring about your end, I will follow," he promised.

"Oh, my love—" she breathed.

William brought his bleeding arm to his mouth, sucked in the smallest bit of his own blood and then lowered his head to kiss her. It hit her tongue and a flooding of visions went through her mind in a flash: William at his birth, as a young child and as a young man. His family, his father, his turning—

The vivid intensity of them, of the agonizing pain and emotion they carried with them forced her to draw away and she began to sob. William held her against his pounding heart, terrified of what might be happening and ready to hate himself, did he just do her fatal harm.

"Oh, William! *Your father*—" His attention perked at her words. "You loved him so very much! What you risked— what you gave for him—"

He raised her face to his, searching her eyes and noting with relief that she was not in any physical hurt from it.

"What do you see?" he whispered, trembling at the memories he still held and of the ones she spoke.

"Everything," she admitted. "I can see it all. Your turning—you did not even have a chance—"

He shook his head, remembering the attack clearly, and all of the pain that had followed—the sharp claws tearing into him, the teeth that had ripped his flesh like burning blades. He still could not believe that he had survived it.

"I did not," he agreed. "Not at all."

Elena buried her face into his chest and wrapped her arms around him to hold on tightly.

"I am sorry, William! I am so very sorry!"

The memories were fierce, William agreed. Unfair and unjust and certainly riddled with suffering unlike anything he had ever known. Of course, the worst of it all was that he had failed his father. There had probably been no saving the man, but William had been robbed of the chance to try, or at the very least to be at his side as the man passed away, and for this he wept with Elena.

After some moments, the wave of emotions passed and Elena remained in William's arms, his hand running down her hair as he placed kisses on her brow. She opened her eyes to look up at him, her hand cupping his cheek and her fingertips feeling the warmth of his skin beneath the scruff.

"Are you not afraid?" she asked him softly. He took her hand and kissed her fingers, and then held them close to his chest.

"What is there to be afraid of, aside from losing you?" Elena warmed at his words.

"Of me. You would risk your life being here with me, when I am like this. Needing so terribly to feed, and now that I have tasted your blood."

"I am not afraid. You would know when to stop."

"I wouldn't—I would be so lost in you."

"You would know," he assured her, drawing her in closely to whisper against her ear. "You would not harm me—your heart will not let you, just as mine will not."

Her arms and fingers tightened on him as he spoke.

"How do you fair now?" he asked.

"I feel that I have the beast inside of me now," she said softly, feeling closer to William than she had before. He growled softly at her words, and tightened his embrace.

"Not yet, you do not," he said seductively. Elena's heart leapt and she drew away enough to see the smiling of his eyes, but she was feeling the burning within and it was igniting within him as well.

"And you will remedy that?" she enticed.

"The moment your strength is again within you."

He looked over her face, her burned hands—the improved change from only a few drops having started.

"It seems that you are immune to my blood," he stated. "At least any undesired effects of it." And Elena sighed, nodded, feeling well enough from it. "Can you take more?"

She smiled softly at his kind offering and when she nodded, he tipped her back with his wrist over her mouth.

"Take it as it falls, my sweet."

The fresh drops landed squarely on her tongue, and these were also full of emotion, but far sweeter and the memories were of recent past. Unspoken words from William's mind crossed into Elena's and her eyes opened to find his on her.

"Well enough?" he whispered, seeing that she knew his thoughts, knew what his heart was feeling. She nodded slowly.

"How long?" she asked, knowing he knew she had seen inside of his emotions.

"Long before we first spoke. And much more so since the first time I set eyes on you," he confessed. His eyes dropped to her hand, and her skin now mending very quickly. He smiled and turned it to show her.

"And everyone was afraid," she said of it.

"Let us not be boastful in haste," he said. "It was only the smallest of amounts."

Elena smiled as well and pushed herself to sit up, some of her strength returning. William grinned at her, but he caught the look she was giving him and brushed his thumb over her cheek.

"Elena—" came his soft voice.

"My beast—" she whispered and his smile grew and shone in his eyes, his hand cupping her face.

"Yes. Yours," he now whispered, lifting her chin to kiss her and feeling the points of her teeth with his tongue.

It was all she could do not to bite him as he kissed her, Elena still tasting his blood and his pulse resounding through everywhere that she touched him.

# Chapter Twenty-Seven

William retrieved Elena's casket from outside of the fortress as soon as the sun rose. Marius had seen to fill it with Elena's clothing, her jewels, and anything else he thought she might want or need, and the entire thing was awaiting William in the back of a wagon. William smirked at the package, Marius's guilt and remorse for it all so obvious in the arrangement that it made William grimace at it. Had they only just left her alone to begin with—

But had they—William might not be so very close with her. No, he knew that it was more than that—most certainly he would not be so close with her and the idea of having to keep his distance now that he knew her as intimately as he did, made William's heart ache.

He took to the reigns at once and headed the wagon back to their little house. Elena would be happy to sleep in her casket again, he was sure. She would no doubt feel much safer from the other Vampyres with it. He reached the house soon afterward, thinking the place to be an unsuitable one for Elena. Certainly she deserved much more than the shack that it was. And upon her awakening, William expressed this to her. Elena did not disagree but instead professed that they both deserved a much more comfortable setting in which to reside. Elena looked over the jewelry that Marius had sent, and after turning them all over to William, she set him off to see what he could acquire for them.

It was by nightfall and by incredible luck that he had found them a larger house—by no means as ridiculously large as the fortress, but just big enough for them both, and Elena's jewels having been priceless, it was an easy procuring and left them wanting for nothing.

But the means by which he had come across it, William hoped Elena never to realize. He knew there would be nothing suitable for her—in neither luxury nor in safety. And again he found himself having to go back to the Vampyres for assistance.

He stood outside of Rigel's manor for a long while, seemingly unseen, but just before dusk, a houseman approached and addressed him.

"My master wishes you to come inside."

William was hesitant to accept the invitation, but reminded himself that it was for his Elena. He had to go. Once inside, William found Rigel awaiting him in his study, sitting behind his desk.

"You have something you wish to speak to me about?" Rigel asked of him, the fascination at having the Lycan in his own home showing in the shine of his eyes, despite the drawn shadow of his abrupt and premature awakening.

William opened the bag of jewels that had belonged to his love and poured them out onto the desktop. Rigel's eyes widened and he tilted his head before picking up the ruby comb she had worn on the night they had met.

"And what is this?"

"I need a home for her. Somewhere safe from the others."

Rigel looked at William for a long moment before he drew in his breath and sighed.

"I would have her here," Rigel began. "She would be safe and that is also my wish for her."

"That will not happen." The firm insistence of William's answer did not surprise Rigel, and yet he could not help feeling his heart drop at the words. "I cannot take the chance that she will be somewhere that could easily turn into a trap. So if you care for her, as you all so claim, I need you to find a place for her, where I can keep her protected."

Again, Rigel thought on it. William wondered if he was going to offer any help at all, and finally Rigel spoke again.

"I do have a house that is not far from here. A day's ride at most. It is secluded, it is safe, and it is not likely that any of the others know of it."

William nodded and pushed the jewelry across the desk to Rigel, but the Vampyre only looked at it, not accepting it.

"I want nothing for it," he began. "It is for Elena."

"And I want no debt, for her or myself. And I'll not have you thinking you may come and go as you please across its threshold. Take it. It should be enough for whatever you have to offer."

Rigel stood, knowing that William was right. He went to a shelf of books and removed one, opening it to take a key from its hollowed out inside. He looked it over and held it for a moment, turning the glinting gold object before he handed it to William. He did not let go when the Lycan went to take it from him.

"Under the condition, that you send word on her from time to time. She is still important to us, no matter what has transpired, no matter her involvement with you."

William nodded.

"Very well."

"And she is still welcome here. Be certain that she knows this."

"I will." And the key was released into his hand.

Rigel gave William directions on how to get there, wanting more than anything to follow him for just a glimpse of Elena, but he knew that he could not go. It had to be enough for now that he knew she was under such protection.

William found the house easily, and made a thorough search of it to be sure it was indeed safe. It was not disappointing in the least and though there had been a fortune in jewels piled onto Rigel's desk, William hoped it was a fair enough exchange for the place. He returned to the little shack of a house and retrieved his lady. Once they had arrived, he led Elena into it, one hand over her eyes and the other on her arm to guide her, letting her look once they were inside the foyer. It was perfect of course: two levels, a lavishly furnished cellar for her berth and hidden hallways within the walls, making corridors for them to easily travel through without coming into the rooms themselves. And for Elena— making it possible for her to go from one end of the house to the next without having to risk getting caught in the daylight. It was not terribly far from the fortress but far enough that the others would not so easily sense her there.

"Your castle," William said to her.

"Our castle," she corrected, and William returned her smile.

"Very well, my darling," he agreed, before he led her to one of the upstairs bedchambers.

"Where you are from—" she began. "Did you live in a castle before you came to me?"

"Hardly," he admitted. "Not in size anyway. But it was, I suppose, to me. A cottage of sorts, on the moors and overlooking the sea. Land forever around it all, green as you please."

"It sounds lovely."

151

"I would take you there, if I could," he offered. "Though I would not wish to be around those I once knew—just in case."

"Yes," Elena understood. "Could I ever go back—it would also be too close for me."

She turned to put her arms around his neck then and let him lift her from her feet in a returned embrace.

"But I should not want to ever go now. You have given us a perfect home."

# Chapter Twenty-Eight

Elena knew that William would be turning again soon—without clock or calendar, she knew it, for he had begun to pace in quieter moments and his brow was drawn when he was not looking at her. She could feel it in his touch on her as though he feared the turning to come before it should and she would be caught in his path.

But she was safe—he knew she would be safe—though perhaps not from her own curiosity, he mused. But even then, he knew she could hold her own and not get careless. And she had seen him at it the one time already—it was not as though she did not know what to expect. Still, it was so very unpleasant and not for the likes of her as far as William was concerned. A damnation worse than her own, he thought.

"Why us, do you suppose?" she asked, interrupting his thoughts.

"Why us for what, my love?" He went to her and took her hands in his.

"For what we now must do. Why me for this quickening? Why you for—well, there is no reason for what has happened to you?"

"No. No reason at all. But for you—" He paused and tucked her hair behind her ear. "You are of that special blood. You were born to do what you do."

"You sound like them, William," she teased.

"It must be true, else they would not have let you live."

She sobered.

"Yes. You are right. It is good that I did not fail them, is it not?"

"For what it is worth. Yes."

"And that it makes it possible for me to be with you—it is all worth that."

"I am pleased to know that, though did you not have to live in such a way—"

"And I would take away your curse as well, could I," she said with a smile.

"There is just no questioning of why, then, is there?" he said finally. "For we would not be, without it."

"No, my love."

# Chapter Twenty-Nine

Elena knew that she should stay away from the fortress. She knew that she should have listened to William and gone to Rigel's while he was negotiating his transformations, though she still feared Rigel's reaction to her being there—to her being with William. She could not go there to him. It was best that she kept to herself—stayed in the forests close to their home, where it was unlikely that the other Vampyres would look for her. And did they try, at least they could not enter the house.

But she could not help being there at the castle now. Just as she had been warned that she would be, she was pulled back to it again. She stood at the gates at the forest's edge, holding onto the bars and pressing her face against the cold metal of them. She sighed. She was thankful that she did not feel the pull to be inside—simply seeing it was enough. She was certain that it was because her coffin no longer resided there.

Elena sighed and closed her eyes as an unseasonably warm November breeze passed. She supposed she did miss the fortress a little—until she remembered that it was the place of her beginning, her first moments of being turned echoing inside of its walls. And then there were the threats, the intimidating promises given to her when she had been living within, and it chilled her. Her eyes opened at the memory and she lifted away from the gate, her fingers still clutching it.

She knew that she was not safe there, that she should not be there, was Nicolas close by, but Elena reasoned that it was the middle of the night—he would be hunting and not likely returning yet.

But her nerves, her instincts were peaked just then, feeling, sensing every single change on the ground and in the air. William was closer than he should have been for it being his time—but he was not the only one.

"*Do you never die?*" Nicolas hissed.

Elena whipped around and saw him in a defensive stance, readying to pounce on her did she give him the chance.

"I cannot stop myself from coming here," she excused, wondering if she would be able to outrace him, though she would have to get away from the gate at her back first.

"No, of course you cannot," he sneered. "Do you miss us, Elena? Your makers? Or is that damnable creature all you know now?"

"William is not damnable. He has done far more protecting of me than you ever did."

"You love him." The accusation came with blunt force, and it occurred to Elena with those words that she did. Her fears of harm ever coming to William, her longing to be caught up in his eyes, his embrace—her needing of him burning hotter than the sun. Yes.

"I do love him, Nicolas."

"You traitor!" the Vampyre raged. "Traitor! *Whore!* The thanks we get for the gifts you have been given—"

"Gifts! Again you talk about gifts—you have given no gift to me, Nicolas! You have condemned *me!*"

"Ungrateful and treacherous whore! Did we not take your life and give you another—*better* life? We gave you such a regal honor—the quickening of our elders—"

"An honor!" she scoffed. "That you yourself have hated every notion of from the very beginning!"

"You would never have been able to withstand his blood had we not—" Elena's heart began to pound at his words. "Oh, yes, I know that you have taken his blood. He may not drink yours but he has gone ahead and infected you—*tainted* you!"

"I am *not* tainted! William has given me gifts as well—"

"Gifts. He has given you nothing of the sort! But perhaps his blood—" And he made to reach for her.

Nicolas was interrupted by a nearby howl. He grinned fiendishly at Elena and she filled with dread. She had half-hoped that William had stayed away, but then she knew that he would not, for he knew that it was so very hard for Elena to stay away from the fortress. She should have gone to Rigel's and begged for him to accept her once again into his good graces. She should have tagged along with William and simply kept hidden while he did his deeds. But he was there now, and Elena could feel him coming closer, so bonded were they. Nicolas took notice.

"Call him here—" he demanded. When Elena refused, he pulled a dagger from within his coat, the blade gleaming in the moonlight but not seemingly made of metal.

"I won't."

Nicolas smirked at her.

"This is silver aspen, Elena. It may just look like wood to you, but it is so much more than that to me."

He stepped up closer to her and set the tip against her heart, pinning her against the gate.

"He will be here any moment," she said, trying to remain calm though the wood felt like a searing hot poker against her skin. "But not because I have brought him at *your* beckoning."

"Good. I have something for him as well—" And from within his pocket, he also removed a pistol. "Silver in this too. Only one bullet, but that is all I shall need."

Elena's heart began to ache then as she wanted to call out to William, to warn him now to stay away, but Nicolas had a firm and steady grip on the dagger and he was a fraction away from plunging it directly into her. But she needed say nothing, for William felt Elena's heart calling to his and he appeared, still as the great wolf that the moon influenced him to be. Nicolas's attention went to William where he stood, utter disgust and disdain blatantly expressed on his face, and much more so as he imagined Elena within the fur-covered and monstrous embrace. Nicolas turned fully from Elena to point the pistol at William and in the moment he no longer held her captive, she rushed to part them, Nicolas's gun going off just as she blocked it and the silver pellet hit her instead.

There was no time to react, for the great beast that was William, swept Elena up with one arm and he fled into the woods with her, putting great distance between Nicolas and themselves.

Elena grew sleepy, for the silver affected her in such a way, attacking the part in her that carried William's virus, and along with it came a dull and throbbing pain. When he felt it safe, William set her down onto the ground, his enormous clawed paw of a hand gingerly trying to lift at the fabric of her dress. Elena's hand went to it as well and she cleared the bloody cloth, the bullet sitting in her chest, just above her heart. It had torn through her skin, lodged itself in, and with her hand shaking so, Elena could not dig it out. She sighed against the frustration and discomfort of it, closing her eyes for a moment. It was then that William's hand came back to her, the warmth and softness of his fur brushing over her skin. Her eyes opened again to find that he sat with her patiently, still trapped in the werewolf and under the controlling moon.

She had one heartbeat of fear but he was doing nothing but awaiting her next move. Her eyes went to his at once, the blue of them still shining, the yellow of the beast glowing in them as well and turning them to the color of the sea. She reached out slowly, carefully and caressed his face, her smile growing when his eyes closed briefly in response and William gently pushed his face against her hand.

The aching interrupted the tenderness of the moment and Elena groaned, the sound making William crouch next to her with concern to observe the wound again.

"I cannot get it—" she began, holding her bodice away. "Can you, William?"

The beast hesitated, but the human side of him was eager to help, despite the clumsiness he had to overcome. William knelt closer to her, and looked at the hole the bullet had made, before he drew a claw swiftly across her skin, opening it up a bit more. With a quick flicking of the nail's point and as the wound filled with crimson, he dislodged it and sent it smoking off of his finger as he tossed it away. The blood spilled from Elena but she could not see it, the only thing on her mind being the burn that the bullet had caused on her lover. She sat up quickly and took his hand into hers, looking over the damage from the silver.

"Oh! Does it hurt?" she asked, but he gave no reply other than a soft, low growl, still not having changed entirely back to his human form, though it had begun. She drew her hand through her blood then, realizing that it was there, and wiped it over his new wound. The healing was quick, the blood steaming at the contact with him, but the pain from it vanished. Elena smiled as he looked over his hand and the surprise in his eyes was unmasked. She made to reach out to him again, but he took her by surprise and jumped at her, pinning Elena onto her back on the ground. She caught her breath, and saw him slowly changing back.

A fire burned in his eyes as he kept her there, waiting for her to speak, expecting her words as he heard her heart suddenly racing. Her hands reached up to William's face, the beast still not entirely gone from him, but still enough there to keep him speechless.

"William—" she whispered, her palms against his cheeks. "This time—please—"

And Elena could hear his heart as well now, the near disbelief hitting her as he scooped her into his arms, still leaning above her and he brought her up to his throat. She could not catch her breath, having wanted so terribly to bite him, and now he was letting her, and Elena grasped William to her. The bite came fast, his great arms tightening around her tiny frame as he sat up with her, letting her drink from him. The heat of his blood straight from the vein was intense, forcing her away from it. William half moaned, half growled, wanting her mouth drawing his blood more, the intensity as intoxicatingly sensual for him. She bit into him once more, taking the blood as it came out, careful not to take much. It was only moments later when at last she had to stop, the sweetness overwhelmingly too much and when she moved away in a rush of shaking sobs, William held her close in his human embrace. They passed quickly, and she pulled away just enough.

"Are you all right?" she asked him, smoothing back his hair and placing kisses all over his cheeks. She checked the bite marks, all having started to close already. William smiled at her, sleepy now but feeling different—rejuvenated.

"Yes, my Elena."

"Did I hurt you?"

"No, my love, you did not."

"Do you feel well enough?"

He did not answer her, but looked down at her to check the bullet wound. He sighed, relieved that it was already repairing itself as well. William sighed again, this time with the greatest sense of relief that the bullet had not struck him, and at the terrifying realization that it could have—certainly it would have been the end of him and Nicolas would have been relentless in his claiming of Elena.

"Thank you, my little one," he said then, his entire heart in his voice. "Thank you—"

"Of course, William. You are most welcome."

"I know that I did not seem close at the time," he began. "But I heard what you told Nicolas—"

Elena knew he meant her confession of her love for him, and she felt her cheeks warm at the memory. She smiled and kissed him.

"Yes. It is true."

"And you know that it is also true," he began, laying her back down onto the ground. "That I am loving you, Elena?"

She smiled, feeling it down into her toes and it made them curl.

"Yes, William."

He dipped his head down to kiss her, feeling Elena smile against his lips as she realized that he was naked and ready for the taking of her.

"Are we safe here?" she queried, not stopping his hands from pushing her skirts up her legs.

"Quite."

"And morning—will it not be here soon?"

"It will. But not too soon."

"Will we make it back before the sun?" Elena was asking as they walked. But William had a different concern on his mind and it showed on his face. Elena squeezed his fingers in hers and it brought his attention to her.

"If the moon shows itself again—" she began. "You did me no harm before—"

"I am still leery of taking that chance," he admitted sadly.

"You will know me—" She promised then with nonchalance, but no sooner had the words come from her, did the moon indeed clear again, pinning William beneath its white glow.

As she had seen before, William's change came on suddenly, silently, all of the pain of it—and Elena could see there was much—held inside until the change had finished, and he let out a howl that shook Elena's insides and deafened her ears. He turned and saw her at once, lurching at her and pinning her against a tree, Elena's arm coming up in time to take his bite.

"William!" she shouted and he froze, recognition for her flooding his blue eyes that had not completely changed to their wolfen gold. They teared as he realized what he had done, and he turned and ran quickly into the forest.

Elena caught her breath after a few moments, and she inspected the bite: bloody as it was, it was little more than a grazing. Her heart calmed and she pushed away from the tree, heading the rest of the way to their little house and quickly for she wanted to take no chance in Nicolas showing. She was only just crossing the threshold when William showed behind her, whirling her around gently and checking her arm, for he well remembered what he had done. It was nothing more than a few scratches by then, the spilt blood dry against her skin.

"I am sorry, Elena!" he whispered. "I knew—I knew—"

"Shush. Do not be silly," she soothed back, raking her fingers through his wild hair. "Perhaps you only wanted to return the sentiment," she teased, checking his throat to see that he was nearly healed.

"Do you not see now? That I cannot control the beast all of the time?"

"Yes, my love. I see that. I will be certain to let you be next time," she promised, still smiling, her eyes downcast.

"Well, you are quite safe now for the rest of this cycle," he assured her, tipping her face up to him. She took his kiss, loving the tenderness of it behind his strength. When she opened her eyes, he was smiling at her, but the first bright rays of sunlight caught her attention and she gasped, jumping forward into his hold. William wrapped his arm around her and lifted her cloak to shield her from the light though he still smiled.

"What's this?" she asked, wanting to know why he looked so unconcerned. He lowered the cloak slowly, just enough to let the sunlight fall on her face. Elena kept her eyes closed tightly against it, but the warmth of it on her skin, not burning, lightly caressing with its rays was heavenly.

"Keep your eyes closed, love," he said softly. "It may still be too bright."

She smiled then and too soon, William lifted her cloak to hide her again.

"Come, my sweet," he whispered. "Time for sleep."

"It is from you that I was able to do that?" she asked, letting him lift her into her casket.

"Yes, my lovely." He stroked her face with his fingers, his expression taking on a serious tone. "But mere moments, Elena. Do not attempt more than the slightest of moments."

"Was it your bite that made that happen?" she asked. William nodded his head but then shrugged.

"Quite likely."

"Not your blood?"

"Perhaps both. I cannot be certain."

Elena remembered then of Nicolas and his attack on them both, and it darkened her eyes.

"What is it?" William asked.

"Nicolas. He will no doubt try again."

William sighed and nodded.

"I would be surprised if he did not. We will have to take care."

"I will not be able to stay away from the castle. You know this," she stated.

"Yes. I do know this. Perhaps you can keep yourself from it until it is nearly time to return home for rest. Then you will not have to make yourself so easily ready for capture."

"True enough."

"He will not stop."

"Yes," she whispered. "Until I am dead, most likely."

"Do be so very careful, my love. I will watch as closely on you as I can. Sleep now, little one. Into your sweet dreams."

# Chapter Thirty

Elena awoke to find that William still asleep in the bed that he had placed next to her casket. She rose and went to his side, knowing that she should awaken him but so peaceful did he appear, she did not dare disturb him. She placed a soft kiss on his lips, sill not bringing him from slumber, before she left their house to feed.

It was a haunting feeling that accompanied her, so used to having William there that Elena felt quite lost without him, though she knew exactly where she was otherwise. She considered going back, paused on her path and pondered it. She had to press forward, so drawn was she again, but this time to Rigel's. She half wondered as she journeyed to his manor, whether it was by her own will or by some drawing of his own. She did want to see him, she knew, despite the resentment he might have at seeing her. But things had not been left with them in such a way, Elena thought. At least, it had not quite seemed so to her. He had to have known of her gratefulness to him, for saving her life, no matter that she had acted unappreciative last they had seen one another. There was not much time for her to ponder it, and less time still to change her mind, for in such a short while, Elena found herself climbing the steps to Rigel's front door, and her hand was falling with her repetitious raps before she could stop them.

# Chapter Thirty-One

When the door opened, Elena felt suddenly frozen to the step. The doorman recognized her at once, bowed and accepted her inside. It was not until she saw the dark of Rigel's eyes as he came to see who was visiting, that she was able to move, and she entered.

"Elena—"

She nodded at Rigel, apprehensive of his feelings for her now and he approached her with caution of his own. He stopped a short distance from her and waited for her to speak next.

"I am sorry to show unannounced and uninvited."

"You need not be, Elena. You know you are welcome here anytime."

She hesitated in saying more, and wished she could form her thoughts into something cohesive enough for Rigel to interpret on his own. He sighed and made the next attempt.

"You recovered well from Nicolas's—*act* on you."

"Yes, thanks be to you."

"And, the episode in the sun—you are healed from that as well."

Elena looked at her hands and showed their backs to him modestly. Rigel could not stand the distance between them then and took steps forward to close it, and take her hands into his to kiss them. Her skin had become softer, brighter and her face was glowing radiantly. He touched her cheek and lost himself in her eyes for a moment, the sudden memory of detail, making him draw away.

"Rigel—?"

"It is said that you took William's blood in order to heal from the sunlight."

"It is true. How did you know?"

"There is very little that can happen in our population that would get past me."

Elena pulled her hands away, blocking other thoughts of William from Rigel. But his eyes shone with intrigue and his questions were so great in number, Elena could not separate them for the reading of them.

"What was it like?" The question came so plainly, so unexpectedly then, Elena was not certain how to answer him. He saw her hesitation and grew embarrassed at his manner of speaking. He nodded at her. "Of course. Not here—"

165

And a bit of his fear swayed as he held his arm out, directing her toward a sitting room. Elena went to it with Rigel just at her heels, he pausing to shut the doors for privacy. He did not move much past the doors, but motioned for Elena to sit comfortably.

"You wanted to know what it was like—" she began, and a youthful interest lit up his ebony eyes. "It was much the same as taking anyone else's blood."

"Only—?"

"Only more intense. More powerful. The images and memories and emotions—"

"Much more so."

"Yes. *Very* much more so."

He thought it over for a few moments, his mouth lilting into a small, pleased smile: one of their own had taken the blood of the Lycan, and nothing had happened to her. *Nothing had happened*—the smile went as quickly as it had come at that. No harm done to Elena—which meant that it would no doubt do nothing to Nicholas, did he try to drink from her. Shame for thinking to put her in such a position filled Rigel and his mood became quite dark. It did not entirely matter that she had survived it, though he was relieved that she had. But there were other concerns to address now.

"You realize that you can no longer safely quicken others."

"But it did no harm to me. It will most likely not do anything to the others."

"But the others are not *you*! You withstood it, but we cannot take the chance on anyone else. The whole idea of having you do the quickenings to begin with—because you were strong enough. No one else that we have knowledge of, can do it. No one, Elena."

"Yes, Rigel. I do understand."

"It did not seem to affect you, but—"

"I understand." She lowered her head. "I am deeply sorry, have I disappointed you, milord."

Rigel could not help softening at her words, though it was a rather grim prospect for the Vampyres.

"It is not I whom you will have disappointed," he assured her. "But the many others who so needed you."

Her head dropped even more and her shoulders felt pressed under weights of guilt. *No—not guilt*, she caught herself thinking. She knew she would never trade what she

166

had shared with William, no matter the honor quickening was supposed to have been for her.

"Please extend my deepest apologies," she requested. Rigel nodded and sighed before he came closer to her and knelt at her knee.

"Have there been any—*changes*?" he finally brought himself to ask. "With the taking of his blood?"

Elena felt the answer on her tongue—*no,* and it came out as such, but the rest she caught before she could speak it. Rigel looked disappointed at the word, for he had been hoping that there would have been more. Such a sacrifice, giving up her ability to help the others, and for nothing but the sake of having shared blood with one not their own. It had saved her, Rigel had to remind himself: whatever was in the Lycan's blood had regenerated her overly well.

"I should go—"

She began to rise but Rigel stopped her, touching her again by his hand taking hold of her arm.

"Do not go—" The pleading tone in his voice stopped her more so than his hold.

"Rigel—"

"There is more," he stated, the curiosity in him for her relationship with William more than he could keep from her just then. "I know there is. Will you not tell me? Elena, please—"

"Rigel—"

"It was more than his blood—what was it? What is it that now makes you glow so? As though you have the very light of the moon within you—?"

But she could not tell him the rest, Elena knew. Could not—or *did not want to*? She was not certain, but the thirst for knowledge of it all from Rigel was overwhelming and it set her in a guarded way. She could not tell him.

"There is nothing else, Rigel," she stated firmly. His demeanor changed, became serious and any fragment there may have been of genuine curiosity in him vanished. It made Elena's heart sink to see that it was replaced with a marked sternness that carried no amity, no tenderness and no tolerance for her.

"Find your way to my door," he whispered with grave disappointment, his eyes no longer willing to look at her, and his arm outstretched, hand pointing toward the way out.

# Chapter Thirty-Two

She knew she should not be there again and William had given her so many sweet warnings of it since the last time, but Elena could not help herself and she vowed that she would not go past the gates of the fortress. But it was nearly dawn now and though her coffin would be calling her back to it for sleep, William's blood had made it possible for her to now withstand brief moments in the sun—there would be plenty of time.

She sighed with contentment, some of her former self having returned since she had tasted William's blood, though she would never be quite the same, still having to take the lives of others. She was grateful that no other Vampyres tracked her down, though Marius made certain to check on her through William when he happened to cross paths with him.

Elena smiled to herself, ready to be back with William now, and she turned away from the gate, heading back into the cover of the trees. She had not gone far when a dark flashing raced by her, catching her attention. She turned to see that it had cleared the gate and made for the castle, but it made a dead stop in the grass. She rushed back to the gate to see what it was, a figure kneeling down with a hood over its head. It became clear to her that it was a person, and noting the time of morning that it was, she knew it could only be one of the inhabitants of the fortress. Drawing up her own hood, Elena crossed through the gate and ran to the figure.

She was stunned to see Nicolas, realizing it was he before he saw her, his eyes closed tightly as the sun quickly illuminated them both with its red morning rays. As she had been before, now Nicolas was, cowering in the light, terror striking at the realization that he was about to be consumed by it. But he quickly forgot of his own impending doom when he opened his eyes and saw her coming at him, his disgust welling up at her great strength and courage, for the sun did not harmfully touch her. She was removing her cloak, and heading right for him, reaching Nicolas and draping it over him protectively before it was too late. His face lifted to hers within the shadows of the velvet, bloody tears streaking down his cheeks from eyes filled with anger and hatred and devastation.

"Why are you here?" he scowled at her, letting her help him to stand and then keeping hold of her arm as Elena led him to the fortress door. She did not answer him until they reached it and he was safely within the darkness of the doorway.

"You would leave me to burn to death, Nicolas. But I would not do it to you," she said. "Even if you did deserve it."

"*Deserve* it!" he spat, tearing her protecting cloak off and throwing it at her. "How *dare* you show yourself here, full of that monster's blood and traipsing through the daylight as though you were never one of us!"

His hand shot out and his clawed fingernails raked across her cheek, leaving four deep red streaks behind.

"Get out of my sight! So help me, do I ever lay eyes on you again, I will end you! And there will be no question of it and no beast to save you!" And Nicolas slammed the door in her face once more.

Elena retrieved her wrap and hurried away from the fortress, her fears rising not for herself—but for William. Always for William. She knew that Nicolas knew—the way to destroying her would be through the Lycan. There was no other sure-fire way to do it.

She felt ill, knowing that some of it was the effect of being in the sun. Certainly she was able to withstand it now but not for long and not without grave repercussions.

She wondered if she was sorry she had saved Nicolas from his death. He had certainly been less than gracious, absolutely indignant to say the least. She was not wrong in having told him he did not deserve it. But she had had to do it—no matter the wretchedness of him, Elena could not have left him to die. It made her head spin to try to understand how she could take lives every night for the blood, and yet she could not justify letting Nicolas walk away unscathed.

Elena reached their house quickly, William catching up with her and checking to be sure she was all right, such was her rush in getting in.

"My love?" he began.

"I am all right," she assured him. "I just need to get into my casket—"

He helped her to it, taking her cloak as she climbed in, already feeling sleep coming on.

"What happened?"

"I saw Nicolas—"

"Did he try to hurt you?"

"No, no. I saved him—he was caught out in the daylight."

"*Saved* him? Elena, why? After what he has done to you—"

She laid her head back and clasped his hand in hers, forcing her eyes to remain open so she could see his.

"Nicolas is a selfish monster, William. But I am not."

William's mood softened at her tenderness and he kissed her fingers before taking a cloth to her quickly healing cheek.

"No, my darling. You are not."

"I would trade the day's sleep to stay awake with you, if I could, William."

"I know you would, my sweet. Sleep now."

He placed a kiss on her lips and Elena was fast into her dreams before he could even safely lock her inside.

# Chapter Thirty-Three

William heard the sound of footsteps approaching the door before the knocking even came. He stood at it for a moment, giving a cautious pause before he opened it with a ready stake in hand. Tavin stood just outside with a red envelope in his outstretched hand, the look on his face most somber in the semi-darkness.

"For Elena," he said simply, taking a step back at the threat of the stake but reaching forward. At the sound of his voice, Elena rushed into the room, keeping just behind William's protective frame. When the Vampyre saw her, his eyes lit up, though he tried to contain his joy at seeing her again with the tone of his purpose for being there.

"Lady."

"Tavin—" Her voice was soft as she took the envelope. "What is it?"

"It is from Rigel."

"Oh?" She began to open it.

"It is your summons."

"Summons?" William asked this time.

"You are to go before the counsel." His darker mood returned quickly at the information as much as it was for his having to deliver it. "They all now, of course, know of your involvement with William, thanks be to Nicolas."

"So?" William put his arm up to shield Elena and to keep her from stepping outside. "And is every one of them against what they do not completely know?"

"Nicolas has made a formal request to challenge her. She must show up, if she wants release from any further punishment—imprisonment, to be exact."

"Punishment?" she repeated. "For what? I have stepped out of their circle, renounced my place—"

"Yes. Many are quite broken over that. But he believes that your relationship with William—as he is not one of our own—poses a tremendous danger to us all."

"But William would never bring harm to any of you! He has not harmed me!"

"I know this, Lady. But it is their decision. As it has never before come into question, they are at a loss as to how to handle your choice. As Nicolas seems the only one to have a real concern over it now, as you seem to be thriving," he complimented, with a happily envious smile. It waned as he

173

went on. "He is entitled to call you out on whatever he believes to be worthy of concern."

Elena sighed, looking over the blood red paper that had come in the matching envelope. It was formal, scripted in beautiful black lettering, requesting her presence in Rigel's estate upon the next evening.

"It does not say so," Tavin began, "But are you to refuse—" He paused, remorseful over the message and he held his hands up to her, though he dared not come closer. "Please, Elena, do not refuse."

"William must come as well."

Tavin nodded simply.

"I will carry your message to Rigel, and return for you on the morrow."

She nodded as well and awaited Tavin's next thought.

"It is good to see you, Elena. You do look well."

"Thank you."

He nodded to them both before he departed and William shut the door again, setting the lock. He turned to Elena and lifted her chin to him.

"Are you afraid, my love?" he asked her.

"No," She only half-believing it herself.

"You have done no wrong. Whatever they mean for you, I will take your place," he promised.

"Do not be ridiculous, William," she said, all seriousness in her tone. "It will not come to that."

"I hope you are right, my love," He embraced her, his concern not wavering. But Elena had as little knowing as William did, and she would only know her fate once she faced the others.

# Chapter Thirty-Four

Rigel's coach arrived to retrieve Elena as it had been promised in the missive he had sent, and Tavin stepped out to assist her in alighting. William prepared to follow her into it, but Tavin stopped him, his hand firmly up like a wall but lacking animosity.

"Please. Do not come—"

"I'll not let you take her without me," William protested. "I do not have any trust in her safety without my being there."

"You may trust me," Tavin assured him. "No one wants to see any ill come to her, and certainly *I* do not. I fear that your coming may put you in a precarious situation and ultimately, that will harm Elena. None of our kind—save Nicolas—have any desires in ending you, William, else we would have done it long ago. I cannot promise you will be safe from his wrath, do you show with us."

"I will not ride with you, but I will still be there," William vowed. "For Elena, I will be there."

Tavin nodded to that, knowing that he could not argue against William's love for her, and Tavin joined Elena inside, letting her lean out of her window to pull William close for a kiss.

"I shall follow within a breath of you," he promised, before Tavin alerted the driver to move on.

When they were alone and en route, Elena sighed nervously and afforded Tavin a glance.

"Anyone can see that you are safe with him," he said. "And that his intentions are pure."

"Then why the need for this?"

"It is law, my dear. Nothing more. Have heart. There are none among us who carry hatred for you."

"None but Nicolas."

"Nicolas is lost to us. That he still walks among us is a trifle to us all, but that too is law."

Elena said nothing more for the length of the ride, the sight of Rigel's manor bringing a comfort to settle within her when they stopped in front of it—until she remembered in what manner she had left it, and her security was replaced with uneasiness. Tavin helped her to the ground, leading her into the house, which was brightly lit and as festive as it had been for the masquerade. The memory of that night made her grow troubled and her arm tightened around Tavin's.

"Easy," he said softly. "Do not let your fear show, and if you can help it, do not feel it either."

She laughed nervously, knowing that it would be impossible to do either. The house was full of many other Vampyres, and every one of them pegged her with their stares as she crossed the foyer, still at Tavin's side and as they entered the ballroom.

"Just answer the questions that are asked of you. Just tell them what they want to know."

The room did not look anything like it had last she was there, aside from the throng of Vampyres within it. It was apparent that there was not a single mortal in attendance and Elena felt for a moment that it truly was best that William was not also there.

At the head of the room, Rigel sat in a tall-backed chair flanked by Marius and David, and two others whom Elena did not recognize, but she assumed by the looks of them that they were also ancients. She smiled humbly at Rigel and Marius, neither of them returning the gesture while David looked on with grave concern, and she realized suddenly how dire her situation was. She swallowed soundly, wondering if Tavin could feel her shaking.

"Careful now," he whispered as he led her to the center of the floor and the others made to clear a space around her, many of them taking seats along the edges of the room. "All eyes are on you."

He released her arm but held her hand for a lingering moment, Elena hearing his thought of wanting to bestow a kiss on it and stay to support her, but he refrained, as he was not allowed to do so, before he let go and backed away to take his place with the others.

The din silenced without prompting, and Elena suddenly felt very alone. She kept her eyes on Rigel, for she could not avoid the pull of his.

"Elena—" he began, all of the former gentleness that he had ever shown her erased from his voice. "You have been brought here this night to stand before all other Vampyres, as you have been found to have consorted with a Lycan."

When he paused and awaited her confirmation, Elena thought her heart had stopped in her chest.

"Yes. This I have done."

A gasp rippled through the crowd, though she felt certain it was news already spread.

"And this you have done though you were repeatedly warned by myself and your makers not to do so, for the possibility of harm that it could have brought to you."

Her eyes went to Marius's then and where his expression toward her upon entering the room had been one of disapproving coldness, it was now nothing short of sorrowful. It hit Elena hard and her throat tightened painfully, for where once she had been quite positive that he would have protected her against anything, she was now certain that he had deserted her entirely.

"Yes—" she whispered.

"And why would you continuously defy this rule?"

"It is simply for my love for him. I cannot will my heart to let him go, and I will not do it anyhow. There is nothing that can stop that."

"It is forbidden, Elena."

"Why, Rigel? Why is it forbidden? Because he and I are seemingly so different—one a Vampyre and one a Lycan, and you believe that is wrong? No, we are not so very different—because neither of us has forgotten how to love and to feel all that is good and all that is bad and that we may know the difference. And it is not wrong and that is not why you forbid it—it is because you no longer feel those things as clearly as we do, you do not understand it and you fear *that*—"

Rigel held up his hand to silence her.

"Enough. It is not for any of us to say what makes your ability to love right or wrong. You are here now at the request of one who would challenge you, based on your unwise choice, and for that we must acquiesce."

When Rigel paused, Nicolas entered the room. He came toward her directly, the hatred and fire in his eyes blazing and Elena backed away until he stopped.

"You know for what true reason you have been called for challenge," Rigel asked her to repeat then.

"Yes," she admitted, trying to steady her voice. "Nicolas superficially believes that my involvement with the Lycan is dangerous to all other Vampyres, and that is why it is forbidden." She lowered her head. "But it is not, I assure you."

"Liar!" Nicolas shouted at her, coming closer but not touching her.

177

"Then it is for your jealousy, Nicolas," she said, forcing herself to meet his eyes with hers. "You hate that I do not love *you*—"

"I could give a damn for your love, Elena! You have brought this monster too closely into our circle—you have compromised the safety of us all, and for your foolish insubordination, you must pay the price!"

In a breath, William had forced his way into the room, but he was kept out of Elena's reach and she from his.

"Because this is the first concern of its kind," Rigel went on, "Elena, you must be made an example of. And Nicolas, as you have called this, you may choose Elena's punishment for consideration."

Nicolas did not hesitate before he pulled his silver sword from its sheath and he pointed it at William.

"*You*! I want her to watch you die by my sword! That is to be her punishment!"

"No!" Elena cried, rushing to step in front of William, Nicolas's sword scraping across her chest, and leaving a crimson ribbon bleeding from it. It smoked and stung her, but she held firm. "Anything else, Nicolas, *please*! Anything else—"

"He dies! There is no punishment more fit for your crime than making you suffer!"

"Please, Nicolas—"

"Is that your decision, then?" Rigel asked Nicolas and the younger Vampyre smirked.

"It is."

Elena grabbed hold of the blade, smarting as it was burning into her fingers and her palm, but she held the point of it steady against her heart.

"Please, Rigel! Please, not William! I will take the sword—not William, this is not his fault! He has never done anything against you or our kind! I should have resisted my heart, but I did not! I could not! This is my punishment—let him be!"

Rigel held his hand up to Nicolas to proceed and nodded, prompting Marius to stand suddenly, just as Nicolas jerked the blade back and it cut through Elena's palm. The release of blood caused a stirring with the other Vampyres, and her reaction to the silver sent a rapid whisper throughout the room.

"Wait!" Marius interrupted, and Rigel turned to him.

"Marius?"

"A few nights past, Nicolas failed to return to the fortress before dawn. Elena brought him in safely before the sun could take him—"

"Oh, Marius, *do not*," Nicolas sneered.

"No, Nicolas! *You*, do not," Marius hissed back.

"And how is it that this was possible, Elena?" Rigel asked her then. "You, having had your own brush with death in the sun." Elena hesitated.

"She has taken blood from the wolf," Marius answered quickly in regard to William, and Elena's heart sank at his giving her away.

"I am aware of that," Rigel began, but questions were arising. "You had no more changes when I saw you last. You said that you were not affected from William's blood."

"I was not truthful with you, Rigel, for I did not know how to tell you—it is not only that," Elena started, but Nicolas thrust his sword at her with force, nearly slicing her again and it made many of the other Vampyres cringe. Elena noticed Sasha amongst the crowd, loyal fear for Elena plainly in her expression as she pushed her way closer to her, ready to take the sword herself if it came to the need.

"He has bitten her as well! It is the only way she could possibly withstand the light—!"

"And so now you can once again safely walk in the daylight?" Rigel inquired of her.

"Only for moments," she admitted. "A few short moments. I dare not try for longer."

"At the risk of harm to yourself, you did this for Nicolas."

"Yes."

David stood then to interject.

"This is *not* grounds for a challenge!"

Rigel thought on this for a moment before he turned to Marius and David and the other two ancients, the lot of them consulting one another in hushed voices. When he turned back to face Elena and Nicolas, his face was darkened and grim.

"Away with your sword, Nicolas," he instructed and Nicolas reluctantly and sharply put it away, awaiting instruction. "You will not touch the Lycan, but it is decided that you may, if you feel that you have been wronged by her, if it is your choosing, put an end to Elena."

179

Elena felt her legs weaken beneath her and she fought their attempt to buckle, as her eyes went to Marius, begging him silently for reprieve, but he would not look at her. David kept his gaze on her, the intense dark blue of his eyes seeming as though they tried to shield her somehow, but Elena was too distraught to try to read his thoughts. She looked at William then, his eyes shining brightly with the pain and love he felt for her.

"By what means?" Nicolas asked bitterly, ungraciously accepting.

"You will drink from her, the Lycan's blood—and all that it may bestow upon you, until she ceases to live. Do you accept this?"

And without answering, he came at her quickly from behind, taking Elena's throat in his hand and choking her.

"*Nicolas*—" she forced out breathlessly.

"Bite your tongue, traitor!" he hissed against her ear. "I shall bite you and I shall take all of the blood *he* has given you, and after three hundred years, I too shall walk in the sun again!"

"*No*, Nicolas—" She gasped as all others looked on, as Sasha took a few steps forward but could come no closer, and Marius with the terror of anticipation freezing him to only watch from where he stood.

"*Yes*, Elena."

Without hesitation, Nicolas pierced Elena's neck and drew out the blood that flowed from it. He could taste the strength of William at once, the poison in it of the Lycan's kind running relentlessly down Nicolas's throat like blades and deep into the pit of his stomach. He wanted to release Elena and draw away, but suddenly he could not. The blood was powerful—too powerful and it agonized and it burned all through him.

"Nicolas, stop—" she whispered, unable to see the terror in his eyes at the realization that something was terribly wrong.

Elena felt dizzied and weak, his bleeding of her taking her strength as it always did. But Nicolas was frozen behind her, and his locked stance became rigid but no longer imprisoning. She turned her head slowly, raising her hands to his arm and he did not budge. Elena carefully drew his hand from her throat, moving carefully, turning to face him and seeing that his eyes had filled with the red of the blood. His mouth was agape, the blood he had drawn dripping from it for he could no longer swallow, and a heat came off of him that was so intense, it was scorching his flesh from the inside out. She moved away from him quickly, seeing the smoke rising from his pores and the blood now coming from his very aware eyes. He was trapped within himself, paralyzed, feeling every bit of his own destruction and realizing why it was happening. And there was nothing he could do to stop any of it—it was much too late for him.

Elena collapsed onto the floor, William suddenly released and at her side to draw her into his arms. He helped her to stand quickly, protecting her from the other Vampyres, as they all began to approach with caution.

"Are you all right, my love?" he asked her, checking her throat and keeping his hands cradling her head. She nodded, hardly able to hold up her head and powerless to help the tears that fell, blood and water alike this time.

They were interrupted as Marius came down at them from the dais, William sheltering Elena with his embrace from him. She turned away as well, but Marius was not there to cause harm, his hands up pleadingly.

"Elena—do not—please, wait—do you not see? It was the only way—"

He reached them, still keeping his distance so as not to scare her further.

"Only way—?" she asked, her voice still weak as she inched further into William's arms.

The other Vampyres began to file in more closely around them, none of them intending any ill will and many of them silently expressing their awe of Elena and curiosity of William. David reached her first with an offered vein, his allegiance to Elena shamelessly displayed to all. He bit his own wrist and let the younger Vampyre drink, not fearing the risks, were there any to be had, for he knew what Elena had faced when quickening him. Truly, it was the least he could do for her.

"We are not able to purposely kill our own," Rigel explained. "For that is a crime far worse than you and William finding one another could ever be. But Nicolas's time had come, for what he had tried to do to you. He could not be trusted, and he could not be allowed to bring danger to anyone else."

"Why did you not just tell me?" she asked.

"Because, sweet Elena," Marius said, reaching out to her but still, despite his desire to, never touching her. "You are not a killer. You would never have done it, even as it was your entitlement."

"And just now—had he killed me?"

"It was not possible," Rigel answered. "We would not have let it go so far."

"But the bite—" William intervened. "You did not know it would harm him—my blood did no ill to her, but has made her stronger."

"True, we would have had a terrible monster on our hands, had Nicolas been able to withstand it. But Nicolas was not Elena. And already we have known that she was quite different."

"That she is," William agreed, still not letting her out of his arms.

"Elena, do forgive us," Marius requested. "Could we have told you—could there have been another way—"

Rigel knelt on his knee before Elena then, his head bowed and every last Vampyre in the room, followed suit.

"We are in your debt now," he said softly.

Elena and William remained in the loving and steadfast arms of one another, the very world of the Vampyres now at their feet, and the smoky ash that was once Nicolas now left in a death-struck, smoldering form of what he once was behind them.